# When Danger Knocks

Ingrid Frank

# Contents

**1**

CHAPTER 1

G ISELE

Monday night.

I reach into the drawer of my bathroom vanity and grab the eight-inch dildo, flipping it in the air before slamming the suction end onto the wall tiles. The bathroom is filled with thick steam from the hot shower, which I'd turned on earlier to warm up. I got carried away scrolling through my phone, and now it's been running for way too long.

Whatever. It's been a long, exhausting day. I deserve to waste a little water before getting myself off and crashing into bed.

I peel off my skirt and blouse, both feeling dirty in that been-in-the-office-all-day kind of way. After a full day of being stuck behind a desk, I still had to drag myself to the grocery store and then haul everything home, trudging up the stairs of my dingy apartment.

I hate this place. What's worse is knowing I bust my ass at a senior position in some fancy corporate office and still barely make enough to afford this dump.

My grand prize after all that soul-sucking work? Cockroaches and cracks in the walls. Lovely.

I snap open my bra and slide my thong down my legs, wishing I had some good dick to keep me satisfied until the weekend. And I mean good—the kind that could pin me against the wall and leave me breathless, rough enough to make me forget my problems for a while.

But this place is so trashy I wouldn't dream of bringing anyone home, even after a night out or a mediocre date.

Not that it matters too much. Part of why I'm working so many hours is because I spend quite a bit of time on my knees in my boss's office. If everything goes according to plan, I'll be getting a raise soon and moving into a nicer apartment before the year's over.

My boss isn't exactly a heartthrob, and the sex isn't mind-blowing, but it's enough to keep me in his good graces. I just have to keep up this illusion of a polished, put-together professional a bit longer.

Keep pretending I'm not a chaotic mess living off take-out until it becomes my reality. Then, I can bring home whoever I want and finally find someone who knows how to wreck me right.

I step into the tub, shivering a little as the cold tiles meet my toes, slick with steam from the shower. For all its flaws, I can't complain about the bathroom.

When I was apartment hunting a few years ago, I saw some bathrooms that looked straight out of a crime scene. At least mine is white, decently sized, and clean enough to stick my toys on the wall without second thoughts.

I rinse off, lathering soap onto my skin before continuing my little session with the wall-mounted toy. As I scrub shampoo into my scalp, letting my pointed nails work out the stress of the day, I hear a thump. I brush it off at first. Living in a busy part of town, random noises are a constant.

But as I rinse out the shampoo and start to reach for another wash, there's another thump—followed by a loud crash. These aren't city sounds; they're too close. My body goes rigid, every muscle tensing as I try to listen past the roar of the water.

I can't hear a thing. My hand shoots out, ready to turn off the shower, but before I get the chance, the bathroom door slams open.

I gasp, clapping a hand over my mouth to stifle the sound as I stumble backward. My heart is pounding in my chest as I collide with the wall, my back sliding against the dildo stuck there. Just my luck—about to get murdered, and the first thing the cops will see is my eight-inch silicone buddy on display.

In a moment of sheer panic, I grab the nearly empty shampoo bottle and unscrew the cap, quickly filling it with water. I shake it up, turning it into a makeshift weapon. If someone's in here to attack me, I'll at least get a good shot of foam in their eyes.

Heavy footsteps echo closer, and I freeze, too terrified to peek out from behind the shower curtain. But whoever's out there isn't in a rush to reveal me. They're taking their sweet time. Whether that's a good sign or a bad one, I can't tell.

I finally risk a glance, peering from the edge of the curtain. All I can make out is a gloved hand, black leather fingers tracing over my lavender bra draped across the sink counter.

Damn me for wishing I had some dick. As I stand in the shower, the intruder's gaze pierces through the steam, locking onto me with startling intensity. He's decked out entirely in black—cargo pants, boots, a sweatshirt, and a hood pulled low.

A ski mask covers his face, with a skull printed on it, revealing only a pair of bright, unsettling blue eyes. The look is almost cartoonishly clichéd, like he's straight out of a heist movie. But those eyes—there's something raw and feral about them.

They're the kind of eyes that make you forget every plan of self-defense you thought you'd learned.

They're blue.

His head snaps towards me when he notices I'm peeking from behind the curtain. I clutch the shampoo bottle like it's a weapon, shrinking back into the corner of the tub, my heart racing.

He steps closer, boots echoing against the bathroom tiles, but he doesn't rush to attack. Instead, he draws back the shower curtain slowly, as if savoring the moment. The sharp swoosh of the curtain fills the small space as he stands there, staring at me, unmoving.

I expect him to lunge, maybe grab me by the throat, but he does nothing. His gaze trails over my naked form, taking in every inch, and for a moment, it feels like I'm being examined rather than threatened.

My fingers tighten around the shampoo bottle, ready to spray it in his face, but he makes no aggressive move. He just watches. There's a bizarre mix of caution and curiosity in his stance, like he's trying to figure me out.

He reaches out, and I flinch, lifting the bottle slightly. His hand hesitates mid-air, almost like he's afraid to scare me off, but then he gently grabs my wrist. He doesn't try to take the bottle.

Instead, he guides my arm down, uncrossing it with a firm but gentle grip. My breath hitches. I can feel my pulse in my throat, and I let my arms drop to my sides, feeling exposed in a way that's both terrifying and strangely thrilling.

The silence stretches between us, broken only by the sound of water cascading from the showerhead. His eyes remain fixed on mine, an unreadable expression behind that mask.

Suddenly, a voice shouts from the hallway, "Heath! We gotta go! This is wrong house. And neighbors called the cops!"

The intruder—Heath, apparently—doesn't flinch. He glances towards the door, then back at me.

His grip on my wrist loosens, but he doesn't let go. "Go," he commands in a low, gruff voice. "I'll see you at the keep."

The other voice protests, "No, we need to leave now!"

Heath's tone hardens. "I said go!" There's an authority in his voice that sends shivers down my spine.

Whoever this other person is, they obey, their footsteps retreating in a hurry. The apartment door slams shut, and suddenly, it's just us. Alone.

The reality of the situation hits me, but the fear that should be coursing through me is overshadowed by an inexplicable rush of excitement.

He turns his attention back to me, drawing open the shower curtain once more. I instinctively cover myself again, but he just shakes his head. "No," he mutters.

His voice is rough, filled with a strange intensity that sends heat pooling in my stomach. Slowly, I let my arms fall back to my sides. I'm fully exposed, my skin prickling under his gaze.

I should be screaming for help, trying to escape, but instead, I find myself rooted in place, my curiosity and arousal outweighing my fear.

Without warning, Heath drops to his knees in front of me, his black cargo pants soaking up the water splashing from the shower. His posture is almost reverent, like he's bowing. "What's your name?" he asks, his voice barely above a whisper.

I swallow hard, staring down at him. "Gisele." I manage to whisper back.

"Mhm, Gisele"

The way he said my name sends a thrill through me, like it's a sacred word. His hands reach up, fingers brushing my hips.

His gloves are off now, revealing tattooed hands with veins that stand out starkly against his pale skin.

I shiver at the feel of his rough fingers gliding over my wet skin. His touch is surprisingly gentle, almost like he's afraid I'll break.

I glance towards the door, half-expecting his partner to burst back in, but there's nothing.

Just the sound of water hitting the tiles and the rapid pounding of my own heart. He traces a path down my thigh, his gaze fixed on the movement of his hand. My body reacts involuntarily, a quiet moan slipping past my lips.

His head snaps up, those wild blue eyes locking onto mine again.

He leans in closer, his breath hot against my skin. "Gisele," he murmurs, dragging a finger along my thigh, dangerously close to where I'm aching for contact.

My body jerks in response, my hips shifting towards him without conscious thought.

Just as he starts to slide his fingers through my folds, the bathroom door bursts open. "Police! Freeze!" a voice shouts, cutting through the haze of lust and fear that's fogged my mind.

I yelp, slipping on the wet floor and stumbling forward. Heath catches me, his strong arms wrapping around my body, pulling me tight against him. He turns us both towards the cop, who has his gun trained right on us, his face a mask of shock and confusion.

Heath doesn't miss a beat. "Whoa, Officer," he says smoothly, his voice calm and oddly reassuring despite the situation. "This is just a bit of role-play with my girlfriend. Isn't that right, Gisele?" His lips are close to my ear, his breath hot against my skin.

The officer's eyes dart between us, clearly unsure of what he's walked into. He hesitates, lowering his gun slightly. "Ma'am, is this true? Are you alright?"

My mind races. I should scream, tell the cop this is a lie.

But the feel of Heath's hand gripping my waist, the way his fingers dig into my flesh—it's intoxicating.

The thrill of the moment takes over, and I find myself nodding. "Heath just likes to go all out," I say quickly, feeling Heath's grip tighten around me. "It's, uh, part of the role-play."

The officer exhales, visibly relieved. "False alarm," he mutters, putting his gun away as a female cop enters.

"Clear in the rest of the place," she says, frowning at the scene.

"Just a sex thing," he explains. She rolls her eyes and walks off, annoyed.

He looks at me one last time. "Be safe. You know who to call if you need help."

Who to call for what? If a man ever broke into my house and touched my pussy? Yeah. Thanks, Officer.

"Sure," I whisper.

The cop nods, muttering something under his breath as he backs out of the bathroom, closing the door behind him.

As soon as the door clicks shut, Heath pulls back slightly, his grip on me loosening. His eyes flick to mine, a dark smile playing on his lips.

The moment they leave, Heath chuckles behind his mask, fingers trailing my skin. "Dramatic, huh?"

"You didn't give me much choice," I whisper back, shivering as his grip tightens, pulse racing.

**2**

— • —

## CHAPTER 2

H EATH

Same night.

The place is an absolute shithole. I almost slip down the damn wooden stairs on the way up—they're rubbed so raw, it's a miracle they haven't collapsed yet.

It's obvious no one has taken care of this building in years, which makes it perfect for rummaging. It has be in the cupboards. Or lockers in one of these houses. We couldn't find the exact house, and I hate the fact that we have to check each one now, like pathetic thieves.

Once inside the apartment, I notice right away that the shower is on, the light gleaming beneath the bathroom door. Neil spins off into the single bedroom, Fran starts searching the kitchen, and I burst into the bathroom, ready to knock out whoever's in the shower so they don't squeal to the cops.

I expect some greasy, gross tenant. Someone who looks like they belong in this ratty apartment building. But when I spot the lavender lace set on the sink, I realize it might be a woman.

A young woman, judging by the purple dental floss she's apparently using as a thong.

God, it looks uncomfortable. Not exactly on my list of things I'd want up my ass.

I pause, hesitating. The things I have to do for this work. But gotta do something to prove it to my dad.

But screw it, she needs to be dealt with.

I rip open the shower curtain, ready to smash her head into the tiles, and I freeze.

Holy fucking hell.

The most stunning creature I've ever seen stands under the stream, clutching a shampoo bottle to her chest.

I reel back, my eyes wide, heart pounding as I stare. Her dark hair is plastered to the sides of her head, trailing down her arms like slick streaks of ink, stopping just below her ribs. She looks like a sparkly mermaid, her gray eyes big and wet, droplets slipping over her freckled cheeks and down her trembling, pink lip.

Is she really going to use that shampoo as a weapon? Smart girl.

I watch her shake, her breath catching as she stares at me.

A gift. She's definitely a gift from the universe. For me only.

I urge her with my eyes to uncross her arms, wanting to see her beautiful tits, and she obliges. A blessing. Such a good girl for me already.

Mine. Mine. Mine.

"Heath!" Neil calls from outside. I draw the curtain shut quickly, hiding my prize from his view. His head pops in through the doorway. "We gotta go. This is wrong house. And neighbours called the cops."

Oh, hell fucking no. I'm not about to leave this specimen behind. "Go," I bite. "I'll see you at the keep."

"No. We gotta go now, man."

"I said go!" He rolls his eyes and disappeared. Good.

Once I am sure both Neil and Fran are gone, I open the curtain again to stare at my gift. She tries to cover herself with her arms, and I beg her not to. I can't help but drop to my knees before her. She is such a beautiful, good girl.

Just as I take her skin in my hands, as I feel her desperate, soaked cunt on my fingers, the fucking cops show up. Of fucking course.

I can't complain too much, though, because my girl drops into my arms, butt-ass naked and heaving. My cock screams against the zipper of my pants as I hold her. I pull her in tight, covering every piece of her that is mine with my arms so the officer can't see. I'd never allow him the privilege.

My dick only gets harder as she plays along with me, telling the officer we are just messing around. We certainly are about to be.

Gisele. My beautiful girl.

I practically come when she says my fucking name. Heath. I decide I must hear her say it again. And again. And again. Preferably while she screams for me, coming around my cock.

Finally, the officer fucks off, and I loose my hold on my girl, allowing my hands to trace along her skin once more, picking up where we'd left off. She shivers and flinch.

"You didn't give me much choice" she whispers. Naive girl. She did it because, deep down, she already knows she is mine, as I am hers.

I ignore her moral dilemma and continue dragging my fingers over her, slipping a hand between her legs. I curl two fingers inside that sweet pussy.

"Oh, god," she moans, her head falling back as she pushes away from me with her arms. My expression harden.

God? Who the fuck is this god she spoke to? I hardly have time to acknowledge the fact that she is pretending to want to get away from me, pushing at my chest though she clenches around my fingers, because I am so fucking upset that it isn't my name which tumbled from her lips.

"Heath," I tell her. Has she already forgotten? "Heath is what you say when you feel this way."

"Fuck." She pushes her palms against me harder, wriggling her slippery body from my grasp.

Have I not been so completely shocked by the gesture, I might've been able to hold on to her. But she slithers away.

What the actual fuck? Why the fuck is she not letting me worship her?

But I know one thing for sure—I'm not letting her go that easily.

GISELE

I slide back against the cold tiles, trying to put distance between us, my bare ass sliding over the tiles. My mind races—there's no way I'm actually considering letting this guy touch me, right? It's clear what he wants, but he's a fucking intruder.

The rational part of me screams to run, to yell for help, but something deep in my gut holds me back, rooting me in place.

He rises from his crouch and pulls a switchblade from his pocket, flicking it open with a practiced motion. My heart clenches with fear, and I have to swallow down a gasp.

Oh, fuck, fuck, fuck. I really messed up.

If I scream now, maybe the officers could make it back in time. But before I can decide whether to shout, he turns away from me.

He grabs the dildo from the shower ledge, and with a sharp flick of his knife, slices it clean in half.

"Hey!" I yell, as the head of my favorite toy lands in the trash. My voice comes out more indignant than afraid, but I immediately regret it. He whips around, a dangerous glint in his eyes.

His knife disappears back into his pocket, but the message is clear: he can bring it out again anytime he likes. He steps closer, each of his boots thudding heavily on the tiles until he's looming over me.

His dark eyes trace my naked form, and I can't help but notice the bulge pressing against his pants.

"A-are you going to fuck me?" I manage to ask, my voice shaking. He shakes his head slowly, the tension in the air thickening.

Despite the fear curling in my belly, I feel an involuntary clench deep inside. The cold floor beneath me sends shivers through my body, and the sound of the running shower fades into the background. My skin prickles with goosebumps as I wait for his next move.

"What do you want, then?" I ask, my voice barely more than a whisper.

"Show me your other toys," he orders, his voice calm but laced with a threat as if it was actually a threat.

For a moment, I just stare at him, confused. Is he serious? What kind of robber is this? But when I hesitate, his hand drifts back to his pocket, where the knife waits. That's all the motivation I need.

Okay, that was definitely a threat.

I scramble up and head for the sink, pulling open the drawer to retrieve a smaller dildo. I hardly use it anymore. He already destroyed my favorite one.

He yanks it from my grip, sticks it to the counter, and slices it clean in half with a swift motion. The pieces clatter into the sink. "The rest," he demands when finished, without even looking at me.

I stumble towards my bedroom, his heavy steps close behind. My fingers fumble as I open the nightstand drawer, grabbing a thin, pink vibrator I'd been meaning to try. He snatches it up and snaps it in half as if it were nothing more than a pencil.

"Seriously?" I exclaim, both annoyed and slightly awed by his strength. But no, I'm pissed off by him.

But before I can react further, his hand shoots out, clamping around my throat. I gasp, staring into his dark eyes, the skull mask making him look even more menacing.

"All. Of. Them." His grip tightens, sending a shiver through me, and I can't hold back a small, pitiful whimper.

His eyes flicker with something dark and primal. He slams the nightstand drawer shut, tossing me back onto the bed.

"I want to hear more of those sounds," he growls, crawling over me, his hand finding my neck once more.

"Maybe if you hadn't destroyed all my toys, I'd have shown you," I gasp, half-joking through the fear.

He smirks, squeezing just a bit harder. "The only thing making you scream will be me. No toys, no pillows, not even your own pretty fingers."

"So... you are going to fuck me?"

"Fuck you?" He leans down, bringing his face closer to mine. "I am going to own you."

Heath keeps his hand around my throat as his free hand forces my legs apart. I stiffen, pushing back against him instinctively, but I can't hold on to the resistance. Something inside me melts at his touch, and I know I've already given in.

Maybe I'm lying to myself, pretending I have any morals left in this moment. But as he presses closer, I realize I don't care. I want this. For reasons even I can't understand, I want him.

He leans over me, a dark shadow blotting out the dim light in my room. I'm spread out before him, naked and vulnerable, his presence heavy in the space between us.

His gaze rakes over my body like he's memorizing every curve, every inch.

Slowly, he drags a finger through my slick folds, making me gasp. A whimper escapes my lips as he dips down again, his touch deliberate and slow.

**3**

— · —

## CHAPTER 3

G ISELE

Then, his hand explores further, grabbing my hip, sliding up my side, until he cups my breast. He squeezes, his
fingers rough as they pinch my nipple. The sharp pain sends
a shock through me, and I yelp, my hips bucking instinctively
into the matress.

I swear I hear a low chuckle rumble from behind that skull
mask of his, a dark satisfaction at my reaction.

"Tell me," he growls, his voice thick with command, "what you
say when you feel like this."

"Heath," I breathe out, the word leaving my lips before I can
think.

"Again," he demands, his fingers teasing their way down my
stomach.

"Heath," I moan, shivering as his thumb circles my clit, a
slow, torturous rhythm that has me arching toward him.

"Again, my Gisele," he insists, his voice dripping with pos-
session.

"He- Heath... Heath" I chant his name, breathless and broken, as his fingers push inside me, curling just right. He slides to his knees on the floor, never breaking contact, his free hand trailing from my throat down to my waist.

He wraps an arm around me, pulling my hips to the edge of the bed, keeping me steady as he thrusts his fingers deeper, his movements confident and controlled.

I glance down, half-expecting him to pull off his mask and taste me, but he doesn't.

His blue eyes stare up at me through the dark sockets of the mask, intense and unblinking, watching every reaction with a kind of hunger that makes my pulse race. God, he looks like he's carved from the shadows themselves, a creature born from the dark.

The coil in my belly tightens rapidly, my body trembling on the edge. I can't hold back—my inner walls clamp down around his fingers, and a jolt of raw energy bursts through me.

I scream, my hands clutching the sheets so tightly my knuckles turn white. My entire body goes rigid, every muscle tensing as I shatter around him.

"Beautiful," he mutters under his breath, like he's speaking to himself, his gaze locked on me. "Fucking beautiful."

I'm panting, my chest heaving as the waves of pleasure slowly ebb away. His fingers slip out of me, and he brings his hand up, glistening with my slickness. He tilts his head, almost as if admiring the sight, before he wipes his fingers on his thigh, his eyes never leaving mine.

There's a flicker of something dark and possessive in his gaze, a promise that this won't be the last time he sees me like this.

I wake up to the obnoxious sound of my alarm at 6:00 a.m.

Groaning, I roll onto my side and pick the muck out of my eyes with the tip of my pointed, black nail. Then, it hits me. There was a fucking intruder in my house last night.

Fuck!

I jump out of bed, opening my nightstand drawer to find nothing but bits and pieces of toys that are destroyed beyond reason. It all comes flooding back. After Heath made me scream like a banshee and destroyed the last of my toys, he simply walked out of the room and disappeared.

I hear the shower turn off, and then a slam. Did he just walk out the front fucking door?

My mind curses my body for the disappointment it feels when he finally walks away. I dwell on his promise as I quickly pull my sheets into place. I am going to own you.

Being the idiot I am, I check the closet and under the bed. I then scurry out of my bedroom, taking in the sight of my kitchen-slash-living room, peeking around the other side of the couch to make sure he isn't crouched there. Finally, I dart to the bathroom, peeling back the shower curtain to find nothing more than my battered dildo nub. He is gone. Well and truly gone.

I shove a thumbnail between my teeth, biting down on it lightly before turning my finger so I can chew off the skin on the side of it. The only things I know about the man are his hands, his eyes, his name, and his voice—well, that and the immense imprint in his pants—and I can't stop fucking thinking about him.

What the hell is wrong with me?

No matter. I decide I'll carry on with my daily routine as usual. Fuck that weirdo.

I change into leggings, a sports bra, and a sweatshirt and head out the door for my typical morning run, my keys tucked next to my boob and my phone strapped to my arm. Everything is completely normal.

It's a spring morning, early April, and while the city has hardly started to warm up, it's at least bearable after five minutes or so of running. But there's one thing. I can't help the feeling I am being watched. Is that noise in the trash can a raccoon, or a freaky masked dildo-destroyer? I look around at the early morning commuters, realizing he could be any one of them.

I don't even know what his fucking face looks like.

I take note of every hand of every person that passes, looking for tattoos and a silver ring. Nothing. By the time I make it home, I'm hardly sure if the whole thing even happened or if I just dreamt it.

Of course, when I return to the shower to rinse off for work and find my lopped dick still stuck to the wall, I'm reminded. It is very, very real.

HEATH

My phone chimes.

Neil: Where the fuck are you?

Me: Busy.

I watch my beautiful gift bounce down the stoop of her apartment building, her ass eating up those blue leggings in a way that almost knocks me out.

Neil: First you come back to the keep late last night, and now you're blowing us off?

So fucking irritating. My phone is distracting me from the fucking view.

Me: Yes.

Me: Fuck off.

I look up to catch the last few seconds of Gisele trotting down the sidewalk, looking around herself suspiciously. Looking around for me, I hope.

Just as her long, dark ponytail follows her around the corner of the block, I make my move. I swing my leg off my motorcycle and leave it standing on the asphalt, my helmet in hand.

Getting into Gisele's place this morning is just as easy as it was last night. The city neglects these parts so much it's almost comical. Except it's not fucking funny at all, and what's worse is that Gisele is stuck living here in these conditions.

That doesn't matter anymore, though. She has me now. Nothing will ever happen to her.

Besides, she'll be in love with me within the week, and then I'll take her away from here.

A cockroach scurries past my foot, and I jump, my breath hitching as it disappears under the fridge. Little fuckers. They have absolutely no right to be squatting here.

I hook up a camera in her bedroom and kitchen. None in the bathroom, and none with sound. I figure I'll at least let her shit and rip ass in peace.

Doesn't matter anyway. If I want to hear her, I'll just tap into her phone.

I whistle as I work, picking up little trinkets and photo frames as I skip around my Gisele's home. She's actually made it pretty endearing for what it is, and I look around happily, taking in the accents I hadn't been able to see last night in the dark.

The disheveled building can hardly keep up against her pleasant decorations: a fern in the corner, beige and cream-colored furniture, wooden utensils displayed on the kitchen counter. She has good taste.

I scratch at my bare jaw and ruffle a hand through my hair as I fall onto her couch, satisfied with my work. Surely, she'll be home from her run soon. It's been a decent amount of time already, and pride blooms in my chest as I note her stamina.

I consider waiting, letting her walk in on me unmasked and hanging around. But I decide against it. She'll see me, all of me, in due time.

My phone chimes again.

Neil: We need to discuss our next target, boss.

Ah, so he's still aware of who I am. I was worried he'd forgotten, given he's made a habit of speaking to me as if he were a friend or colleague. Even though I am not the main boss. This dipshit is the son of my father's very close friend. So I have to keep him.

Me: I'll be there in twenty.

Me: Asshole.

Neil: Love you too.

I stand from my seat and undo the fly of my pants, thinking back on the way Gisele looked last night, running around the apartment naked and terrified, covered in goosebumps and lust.

Never in my life have I ever seen two tits so perfectly hard, nor curves so deliciously wet and inviting.

She, as a whole, is absolutely breathtaking. Stroking my cock from base to tip, I silently reconsidered staying until she gets back but once again decide against it.

I move my attention to the head of my cock, blasting it with short, quick strokes and holding my free hand beneath it, catching my own cum as I groan. I squeeze my dick into my palm like a sauce packet and manage to get my pants back up around my hips, leaving them undone for now.

I parade around her house one last time, dipping my finger in my cum and leaving little gifts for my girl. A few drops in the milk I imagine she'd be using in her coffee, a smear on her pillow so she can smell me as she takes her beauty sleep, a bit in the crotch of her underwear so she will walk around with me all day.

When my work is finally finished, I grab my helmet from the kitchen counter and spin out the door, giggling to myself.

**4**

**CHAPTER 4**

# G ISELE

I burst through my apartment door, practically tossing my laptop bag onto the kitchen counter. My high heels are off before I can take another step, and I let out a groan of relief as I peel them away from my sore feet.

God, the things I put myself through to impress my boss—it's almost pathetic.

I dump my reusable coffee cup in the sink, followed by a couple of Tupperware containers that had once held my sad attempts at healthy snacks.

I eye the pile of dishes and instantly decide: no way I'm dealing with that tonight. I'm way too tired for this shit.

Instead, I lean over the counter, forehead pressed against my folded arms. The weight of the day is heavy, and I can't ignore the gnawing feeling that my so-called perfect life is just a fragile illusion.

Great job, great lifestyle, great image—all of it looks flawless from the outside. But inside? I'm drained, running on fumes.

I push off the counter, dragging my feet toward the bath-room. As I step forward, a small brown roach darts across the floor, and I flinch. I'm not even shocked anymore; these little bastards are part of the deal when you live in this neighbor-hood.

I barely have the energy to be disgusted at this point.

I strip off my office clothes on the way, stepping out of my skirt and unbuttoning my blouse. The steam of the hot shower is already filling the room as I step inside. The heat wraps around me, loosening the knots in my muscles.

I tie up my hair, glancing over at the silicone dildo still stuck to the shower wall. I haven't had the heart to take it down. I'm so sad that he is gone. A love lost.

HEATH

The door creaks as I open it, but my girl probably doesn't hear. She's in the shower, and I am much quieter than my idiot brothers when I want to be. I've been down on the street watching her on my phone.

When I see she disappears into the bathroom, the only place my cameras can't see, I know I have to get up here in time for the in-person show.

Once in the kitchen, I open the pack of roach traps I bought today after leaving the keep and pace around her apartment, leaving one under the couch, another under the fridge, and then one under her bed.

This is my Gisele's apartment. No one else's. The bugs don't deserve to share this space with her.

I spot the dishes in the sink and wonder if I wash them, will the shower scald her? Probably. The place is such a shithole, I'm sure the temperature controls are all connected.

I decide to wait, though I smile at the dirty coffee cup among the containers. Good girl, drinking me like she should.

Judging by the enormous dick on her bathroom wall, which is not my own, I figure my gift uses shower time to touch herself, and I'm not about to let that happen.

It's a good thing I'm so close by, or I might not have gotten upstairs in time, and she might've come without me. Oh, the humanity.

I walk to the bathroom and whip the door open. Her little yelp sounds from behind the curtain. Something tells me she's already started.

My boots eat up the distance between the door and the tub, and I rip the curtain back to find her laid out on the floor, a hand between her legs.

I bend down, my sweatshirt soaking under the water, and grab her by the neck. "Very, very bad girl." I shake my head, wishing I could rip this fucking mask off and nibble every inch of her.

But not yet. I want my reveal to be grand. I wanted her to fall to her knees at the sight of me as I did her.

"I'm sorry," she chokes as I rise and lift her in the air.

I bring her nose to mine, looking down at those full lips, desperate to take a bite.

"What did I tell you?"

"Heath!" she cries in protest, her feet hardly touching the tub, I have her up so high. Well, to my height, but it is high enough that her toes scramble for purchase.

I flip her around in my hold and press her back into me, fishing her messy bun and bending her just enough that she is facing the half dildo on the wall. A reminder. "What the fuck did I tell you?"

"Not even my own fingers," she rasps, her body squirming against me.

I hug her tight against her attempts. She has such a good memory. "Do you want to come, pretty girl?" I ask, nuzzling my nose behind her ear and pressing her body along mine.

"What are you doing here? I'm going to call the cops if you don't stay away!"

Silly girl. She is still in denial.

"Shh-sh-sh." I kiss down her neck and shoulder, damning the fucking ski mask between us as I calm her down.

"I'll forgive you this time, my gift."

"I don't want this!" she cries out. "I don't want you!"

My entire body stiffens, my lip curling. How fucking dare she say that to me?

I spin her around and step into the shower with her, pressing her against the wall and dropping my face to hers, heedless of the fact that Iam getting soaked from head to toe.

"You wound me, little Gisele." I look down at her heaving chest, her-nipples taught and her body trembling. "You do want me. I make you feel good."

I reach a bare hand to her tit, squeezing the hard peak between my pointer and thumb.

"I dare you to say it again. Tell me you don't want me."

She moans, her head tilting back. "I don't want you."

I shake my head. I don't believe her. I drag my fingers from her chest and slowly draw a line down her body until I reach the sweet spot between her legs. Denying her the pleasure of my fingers on her clit, I touch just around it and repeat, "Tell me you don't want me."

"I don't," she whimpers, writhing against the wall. "I don't..."

Stubborn girl. Fucking liar. That makes me angry.

"Fine." I bite, pulling my hands away and stepping out of the shower. I cross my arms and stand still, watching, waiting for her to continue washing herself.

My forehead burns with rage, and my heavy clothes drip onto the floor. My girl is not easy to deal with, but I remind myself that her strength is to be loved and appreciated.

She slowly stands up from the wall, wrapping her arms around her ribs. "What are you doing?"

"You don't want me tonight."

"Then get out"

I almost smile at that. She's a terrible actress. She wants me to stay.

"So you can touch yourself again?" I shake my head back and forth. "Finish your washing."

GISELE

I stare at the masked man in my bathroom, his stance strong and arms crossed. His damp clothes cling to him, revealing a tight, broad figure and—fuck—that imprint between his thighs.

My pussy is absolutely throbbing. I am right in the middle of attempting to get myself off old-school style when he barges in.

And there is something about him. That thing he provokes in the pit of my stomach that I can't quite pin. It makes me gush on sight.

I do want him. Every damned and damaged part of me begs for him. But I can't possibly be so fucked up.

"Can you use the shower and the sink at the same time?" he grumbles after a short silence.

My spine straightens. "Excuse me?"

"Can you use the shower and the sink at the same time?" he repeats with a bit more fervor.

"Uh, yeah. Sure." My eyebrows pool in the middle of my forehead in utter confusion.

Heath stomps out of the bathroom, obviously totally frus-trated with me though I can't see his features, and I almost giggle. He's quite literally gotten grumpy over the fact that I said I didn't want him.

What the fuck? He is a stranger who broke into my house. Is it so horrible of me to say?

No more than a few moments later, he returns; my coffee cup, Tupperware containers, and sponge in hand. He drops everything in the bathroom sink and begins washing my fucking dishes.

Oh, this guy is a total fucking nutcase.

"Don't do that here," I insist. "It'll smell."

He shakes his head. "Smart girl. Trying to get me out of here so you can touch yourself."

At that moment, I realize. Just because he wears a scary mask and breaks into houses, doesn't mean he isn't just a fucking guy. An obnoxious guy with an evident attitude problem.

And I've dealt with plenty of those. I cross my arms tighter and sink into my hip, ready to reprimand him as I have many before.

"Excuse me, this isn't your fucking house," I bite, moving my neck at him like an ostrich. He stops, dropping the sundries in the sink and slowly turning off the water. "You can't just barge in and clean up like you live here."

**5**

**CHAPTER 5**

G ISELE

His head turns to me steadily. It's honestly a little terrifying. "Then what would you rather I do?" His whole body turns away from the sink to face me. "I have tried touching you. I have tried cleaning for you."

"I want you to get the fuck out!"

A low, furious growl sounds from beneath his mask, his head cocking to the side like a deranged animal. "You forget yourself, Gisele."

"Fuck! You!" I immediately step out of the shower and march right up to him, my wet feet slapping the tiles. "You are the intruder in my home!"

I place both hands on his chest and shove. He falls back only a casual step. His reaction is not what I expect.

He reaches both hands to the hem of his soaked sweatshirt, pulling it up slowly. First, I see the "H" above his waistband, then a whirl of tattoos. Vines and roses crawl up the side of his abs and melt into swirls and varying designs. He pulls the fabric up further and further, and I catch a glimpse of a skull, some knives, an hourglass... Fuck, the man is all lean muscle and black ink.

Finally, he pulls his arms through the holes and shucks off the garment, leaving his mask in place. "Do that again," he bites. A threat. That is most certainly a threat.

I pry my gaze away from his perfect body and shove him again.

Fuck, the feel of his skin under my fingers is deliciously hot.

I push again, and his abs flex at the impact. Shit.

I back him up inch by inch as best I can toward the bathroom door. On my fourth shove, he grabs both my wrists in one hand, pulling them up so high I can hardly gain my footing. I cry out in pain.

"Don't forget that I can simply take what I am so generously offering you, Gisele. If I want to fuck you, understand that I will. If I want you to come for me, understand that you will. You are going to fall in love with me. Whether or not you want to fight it is entirely up to you."

"Why the fuck would I ever fall in love with you?!" I spit, twisting in his hold.

He chuckles. "Because I'm a good person, and I'm handsome, and I make you scream."

"Ha!" My head would tilt back with laughter if it weren't caught between my arms. "Good people don't break into other people's homes, and handsome people don't hide their faces."

"So you admit it," he says, tilting his head to one side. "I make you scream." His gaze drops to my tits for a long moment, filled with amusement, and then returns to mine.

Fuck, my chest is heaving, my legs clamping together with desire. It must be the adrenaline. It has to be.

But whatever it is, Heath sees it in my eyes, sees it in the way I lick my lips as I steal one more glance at his bare torso. He gathers me up in his arms in an instant, wrapping my legs around him and slamming my back against the wall.

And I let him. Oh, fuck, I let him.

"Do you want my fingers in your pussy, baby?" he breathes, his noseon mine as I grab his head in my hands. I nod, a squeaky, little whimper escaping me.

He groans as he places his hand over my cunt. "You're so desperatefor me, aren't you?"

Again, I nod, wishing I could kiss him through the fucking maskbut not daring to peel it off.

I am not quite ready to know what I'd find underneath yet. Heath's fingers rams into me. It takes him mere seconds to work meup to near orgasm, and I ground my hips against him, begging him, needing him.

"Oh, god!" I moan.

"Heath," he insists, slamming his hand into me hard.

I scream at the impact. "It's Heath!"

He slams into me again. "Heath!" and again."I'm sorry, Heath," I whimper.

"Yes, Heath." he repeats. My clit stings from the way his palm whack it, my hips chasing the inevitable.

He follows my face with his mask, his nose never leaving-mine. "Much better."

"Yes, Heath, yes..." I chant as my pussy pulls tight, closing around his fingers. I moan and writhe, and he follows every little movement, eating up my energy through his dark clothing, sucking me dry like somekind of demon.

Finally, I slump against the bathroom wall, clinging to my intruder like a lazy, little sloth. He kisses the side of my head through the mask as he carries me back to the shower and set me down on the bottom of the tub.

Stacking my hands on the edge of the porcelain, I rest my chin on them and watch as he turns away from me, pulls his mask out only the slightest bit, reaches his fingers in to, I assume, suck on them, and returns to washing the dishes.

What a weird fucking man.

GISELE

I walk into the office building the next morning, finally able to take a sip of the coffee I brought from home. It was far too hot for the entire subway ride here, and now, it's the perfect temperature.

Dylan, my boss, is already sitting on my desk in my private office when I get in. He looks effortlessly handsome, perched casually on the corner, flipping through the stack of meeting notes from yesterday.

His thick brows raise when he notices me, his brown eyes as inviting as ever, his wavy black hair tousled but neatly styled, backlit by the window behind him.

"Sir," I greet him, hanging my jacket on the coat stand by the door.

"Mmm, I love it when you call me that."

"How inappropriate of you to say," I tease, walking towards my desk and setting down my laptop case. I offer him the cup of coffee. He takes a sip before passing it back to me, and I bring it to my lips.

Dylan's a decent guy, and despite our... less conventional interactions, we make a good team. He's the type who's easy to work with—calm, passive, a little too passive—but that's not always a great thing, not in the office, and certainly not in the bedroom.

But the passive thing isn't just in the office. It's everywhere. In our so-called "hook-ups," he's... well, there, but not exactly fiery. Not the type to chase me around the woods or drag me against a rock, even though, sometimes, I fantasize about that.

And while I'm sure Dylan knows what's going on between us, he never complains. I don't either. It's convenient.

"Tell me you've come up with something mind-blowing for Wixlon next week, my lovely creative director," he says, breaking my thoughts.

I scoff, already bracing for the inevitable disappointment. Wixlon's an up-and-coming office supply distributor trying to promote their new line of state-of-the-art filing cabinets. How the hell am I supposed to make filing cabinets sound remotely interesting? Not even the most creative mind could pitch something like that without dying of boredom.

"I'll take that scoff and that silence as a no," Dylan observes, not missing a beat.

"I might need some inspiration," I respond, pouting my lips and pushing my chest together with my arms. "My life's so boring." Well, my sex life with Dylan's even more boring, but it's better than nothing. Besides, the guy does have some influence over my paycheck.

"Well, I believe I'll need to cancel my two o'clock."

I grin. "And have you talked to your superiors about my compensation, my handsome boss?"

"Campbell," he warns, his tone suddenly more serious. "I'm doing what I can."

I doubt it. "What I can" in Dylan-terms usually translates to "I'm doing the absolute minimum because tough conversations give me anxiety."

I sigh, letting him know just how little I believe him. "Fine, fine."

He hops off my desk, his perfectly tailored suit making him look like he just stepped out of an ad, and saunters toward the door.

"I'll see you at two," he says over his shoulder.

I watch him go, rolling my eyes once he's out of the room. Once I'm alone, I sink into my chair, opening the laptop in front of me. The sight of my overflowing inbox makes me briefly contemplate throwing the whole damn thing out the window, but I can't.

I need to work. Rent isn't going to pay itself, and Cockroach Lane isn't exactly cheap.

Suddenly, my screen lights up with a text notification in the corner.

Unknown: Campbell.

Unknown: Pretty name. Hope you aren't too attached to it.

My heart races, my pulse quickening. Who the hell is this? Is someone watching me? My legs start to shake, a cold sweat prickling at the back of my neck.

I open the chat.

Me: Heath?

Unknown: By the way, if you go to that 2:00, that puffed-up fucker will fare much worse than your little toys.

I freeze. What? I glance around the room, paranoid, trying to shake the unease creeping into my bones. Is someone out to get me? Or is this some sick prank?

Unknown: Are you after a raise?

Unknown: I'll see to it.

Me: What the hell do you mean?

Unknown: Just trust me. Can you do that?

Me: Over my dead body.

Unknown: Bad girl.

Unknown: I hope he enjoyed his sip of coffee. I added a little extra something to your milk.

My hand flies to my mouth, my stomach twisting in knots. Panic surges through me as my fingers tremble while I type.

Me: What the fuck did you do?

Unknown: Drink up, baby.

Me: Are you watching me?

The message lingers on the screen, but no reply comes. Every second that passes makes the air feel heavier, like I'm suffocating.

I should tell someone, but what would I even say? How do I explain this? And why am I still thinking about those eyes?

**6**

**CHAPTER 6**

G ISELE

Minutes drag on, but no response comes. I stare at the coffee sitting innocently on the corner of my desk, the weight of uncertainty settling in.

With a frustrated sigh, I snatch the cup up and stand, only to pause, wondering if I'll even make it to the bathroom in time. What if whatever Heath slipped in starts working before I get there? I wouldn't be shocked if it knocked me out cold in front of reception.

Maybe that wouldn't be the worst thing. At least I wouldn't have to deal with the growing pile of emails waiting for me.

The ringing of my laptop jolts me out of my thoughts. An incoming call from Unknown.

I put the coffee back down, my hand shaking as I swipe to answer, clutching the edge of my laptop like it's the only thing keeping me grounded.

"Baby," Heath's voice crackles through the speakers, rough and full of that strange, hypnotic authority. I almost gasp at how instantly captivating it is.

A few hours and I've already forgotten how easily I get lost in it. No wonder I've let him pull me into his web.

"Heath, this isn't funny," I manage, trying to keep my voice steady. "What did you do to my coffee?"

"I would never hurt you, baby," he says, the words almost sugary. "You're my beautiful gift."

"What the hell does that even mean?" I snap.

"I know you're feeling the same way as I do."

"I don't feel shit."

"Don't worry, I'm not watching you right now." He sounds too pleased with himself. "I only tapped into your phone, listened to what you were up to. I promise." His voice carries that same cocky sweetness as if he's trying to smooth things over, but I'm not buying it.

"Who the hell are you?" I demand. "Where the fuck did you even learn how to do that?"

"YouTube," he replies, almost chirping with excitement, "Five minutes craft"

I push my forehead into my hands, a heavy sigh escaping me. There's no way I'm ever going to get a straight answer from this guy.

"God," I mutter under my breath, slumping back into my chair. "I am so thoroughly fucked"

"Not yet, baby," Heath teases, the words dripping with dark promise. "But you will be. And in case you forgot, I told you not to call out for him. If you're fucked, it's because of me, and me only."

I roll my eyes so hard it almost hurts.

"How do you know God isn't a woman?" I throw back, not even caring if it makes sense.

"Then you may not call out to her. You may not call out to them. You may not call out to any-fucking-one besides me. Do you understand?" His tone has shifted, deeper now, more demanding.

"Big talk for someone who's barely touched me," I mutter, not expecting him to respond.

But he does.

A low, evil laugh rumbles through the line. I can almost picture his face, his head tilting back as he revels in my frustration. "I know you're desperate for me, baby. Don't worry. I promise I'll fix that soon enough."

The call ends abruptly, leaving me staring at the screen in disbelief.

"Wait!" I blurt out. "The coffee! God, what did you do to my coffee?"

The anger wells up, but it's quickly smothered by a sickening mix of curiosity and fear. I want to drink it, but now, I don't know if I dare.

Before I can even think, my laptop chimes again.

Unknown: I came in it :)

HEATH

I snap my phone shut, a quiet chuckle escaping me just as Gisele's screech begins to leak through the open line. She's not going to drink the coffee now, I know that much. But it's too late—she's already had a few sips. That's enough for me. The rest is just a bonus.

I can't help but think about Dylan, her boss. He probably took a sip, too. That thought doesn't sit well with me.

The jealousy surges, like an electric current. I hate him, and I know she's messing with him, provoking him—asking for his "inspiration" as if he has anything valuable to give her. She doesn't need his advice; she needs mine. I'll make sure she gets it.

I glance at the clock on my wrist—9:30 AM. God, it feels like hours before I'll be able to see her again. I can't sit here and wait until 2:00 PM to get this done. I need a distraction.

I take in the cold, looming stone walls of the keep. The place is dead. It's meant to be a holding area, a place for cages, but we don't use it for that anymore.

Our real captives are kept in the new wing, and this part of the building has become nothing more than our private headquarters. It's not the worst place to be, but I'd rather be somewhere else. The walls are too quiet, the air too still.

I watch Neil and Fran argue over the plans for the next month. It's pointless, really. The small jobs, like Gisele's place, don't bring in enough money. Sure, I got my hands on the best gift I could ask for, but a few broken trinkets won't fill the coffers. We need something bigger, something better.

I stand and cross the room, shaking my head as they keep bickering.

"Stop," I growl, feeling the frustration build.

Neil slams his fist on the table, his voice rising. "We need a new partnership. Heath, you really need to talk with your father"

"No," I answer, sharp. "The cops are on our tail. We can't take more risks right now."

Fran chimes in, agreeing, "The hits were too close together. We fucked it up, but now we need to lay low."

Neil glares at him, slamming his hand down again. "His father can easily handle it. He got connections that he never told him about. Laying low won't get us any money!"

"Neither will getting caught, dumbass," Fran shoots back, teasing him with a raised finger, "If we caused any silly troubles, he would kill us all."

I sigh, rubbing my temples. "Both of you, shut up. We're laying low. I'll think of something. No need to bother Dad for this. We'll talk again next week. Got it?"

Neil shoots me a glare, but he knows better than to argue.

I wave them off. "It's done. Now get out of here."

I leave them to it, heading down the long, cold hallway toward my office. Finally, some privacy. My mind is on Gisele, on Dylan, on what I need to do next. Her boss is an idiot.

I don't even care if she's toying with him—it's cute, in a way. But it's not going to last. Not when I'm done with him.

I sit down at my desk, flipping open my laptop. I type "Gisele Campbell" into the search bar, scanning through the results. Creative director at a marketing firm. She's good at what she does, no doubt about it. Promoted two years ago. A senior position, yet still struggling to afford a nice place? That's odd.

A picture of Gisele pops up, looking far too perfect in that stiff professional pose of hers. Next to it is Dylan's picture. His smile is too smug. It makes my blood boil, but I ignore it. This is business.

I don't waste time. It's easy to hack into their company's system. Emails, contact lists, shared folders—all of it. I dig through Dylan's inbox and find the CEO's contact.

A few quick strokes, and I've drafted a glowing letter of recommendation for Gisele. I paint her as the perfect employee: driven, talented, ambitious. Then I send it to the CEO.

I don't stop there. I know Dylan will be the type to open an email from his boss without hesitation, so I send him one, too. The email is bugged, a little present for him to enjoy.

I don't even have to wait long. A minute later, the read receipt pings. I know his computer's been compromised, just for a moment. Nothing permanent, but it'll be enough to make sure I hear back from the CEO without interference.

Once that's done, I quickly delete all traces, wiping everything clean. I'm done planting seeds for her future. Now, I turn to the next task.

I reach into my desk drawer and pull out a wad of cash—I have a plan, and it's happening now.

Hours later, I find myself standing at the base of Gisele's office building. It's a monster of a structure, far more impressive than my own headquarters. I run my hand down the front of my new suit. I glance at my boots—they'll have to do. I didn't need to buy new shoes. But I did.

I shove my hands into my pockets and step through the revolving doors, ready to make my move.

**7**

— · —

## CHAPTER 7

G ISELE

"Miss Campbell." Carly's voice breaks through the quiet of my office. She stands in the doorway, a curious frown creasing her forehead. "There's someone at the front desk. Wants to talk to a rep. A potential client, maybe?" She shakes her head slightly as if confused by the whole situation.

I raise an eyebrow. A walk-in? That's odd. "I'll be there in a minute," I reply, gathering the clutter of papers scattered across my desk.

I neatly pile them up and slide them to the top right corner, then stand up. As I head for the door, I smooth my dress over my hips and tug my hair loose from behind my ears, fluffing it a little. I've been hunched over my work for hours, and I don't want to look like it.

When I reach the reception area, I see him. Tall, sharply dressed, his hands stuffed in his pockets, standing with an air of indifference. Carly, on the other hand, is practically fawning over him, which makes me snicker inwardly. He's undeniably handsome—too handsome, actually. His short, jet-black hair is styled perfectly, his jawline cutting through the air like a blade, and his nose is straight, almost unreal. He notices me and turns, and I freeze in place.

There's no mistaking those eyes. The same pair I've seen in my dreams and nightmares. They're bright, deep, and they burn through me in an instant, drawing me in like a predator stalking prey. I lose myself in them for a moment, caught in the intensity of their gaze, before he speaks.

"Miss Campbell, I presume?" His voice is smooth, like velvet over steel, as he extends a hand toward me. The tattoos on his arm peek out from beneath his sleeve, and I notice a silver ring on his finger. "I hope I'm not intruding, but I thought I might squeeze in for two o'clock. Is there a chance you have time?"

"No," I spit the word out before I can stop myself, turning swiftly and heading back to my office, my heart pounding in my chest. As I walk away, I hear Dylan emerge from behind his door.

He starts speaking about something—probably another issue with his computer—reaching a hand toward my shoulder. But I'm too distracted by the man standing in front of me to listen. Dylan's words fade into the background as I glance back over my shoulder to see him—Heath—following me with a confident stride.

I don't even know what to make of him anymore. This whole situation is insane, and he's making my blood boil for all the wrong reasons. God, he's beautiful. Crazed, but beautiful.

"Who is that?" Dylan whispers, his eyes narrowing as he looks past me at Heath, who's walking toward us with an almost predatory smile.

"No one," I mutter, my voice barely a whisper.

But Heath isn't done. When he reaches us, he extends a hand, his smile widening. "You must be Mr. Jones," he says, his voice dripping with charm. "Heath Steinfeld. How did my dick taste?"

Dylan stares at him in confusion, a mix of disbelief and shock on his face, while I almost choke on the air around me.

"I said, Heath Steinfeld, sir. Of Howard, Dick, & Pace. We just opened an office downtown, and we're looking for a marketing team. I thought I'd stop by to see what you've got." His words are too smooth, too rehearsed. He's making a mockery of this entire thing.

Dylan's brain finally seems to catch up with him, and he gives a quick, fake grin. "Of course! Oh, do speak to Miss Campbell. She knows everything. She's my favorite," he says, patting me on the back with an awkward chuckle.

Heath's eyes widen, an eyebrow arched as if testing the limits of the game. "Oh, is that why?"

"Heath!" I practically shout, my voice a mix of exasperation and disbelief. I clap my hands together, trying to cut off whatever more ridiculous comments Heath might have planned.

"Mr. Steinfeld," I correct myself, forcing a smile that's anything but sincere. "Follow me."

I motion toward my office, trying to act calm even as I can feel the anger building inside. How dare he show up here like this? And why does he have to be so goddamn gorgeous? It's infuriating.

I storm into my office and spin around, crossing my arms. I can hear the door click shut behind me, and the next thing I know, I'm facing Heath, fury flashing through me.

"What the hell do you think you're doing?" I snap, my voice sharp with frustration.

Heath just grins, and I can see that familiar, manic gleam in his eyes. He takes a step closer, groaning softly as his eyes rake over me. "You look so pretty, baby. All dressed up," he murmurs, his hands finding their way around my waist.

He pulls me closer, his gaze never leaving mine, "Do you think I'm pretty?"

Pretty? The man is the most stunning person I've ever laid eyes on, and it's unfair. He doesn't even try, and yet it's like he's been made to break hearts and ruin lives. I swallow hard, but I can't form words.

"You think I'm pretty." he teases with a knowing smile, clearly satisfied by my silence. "Thank you, baby."

"Heath Steinfeld," I scoff, my lips curling in disbelief. "Is that even your real name?"

He tilts his head back, as if savoring the question. "Very much so. Say it again," he demands, the request bordering on playful and possessive.

I click my tongue, irritated by his cocky attitude. "Aren't crime lords supposed to be discrete about their identities?"

He lets out a loud laugh, shaking his head. "I wouldn't exactly call myself a crime lord, per se."

I hold up a hand to stop him. "You need to leave."

But Heath isn't done. He laughs, and the sound is dark and low, sending shivers down my spine. His grin spreads wider, and his eyes seem to glow with mischief.

He reaches for the hem of my dress, running a finger up the inside of my thigh. Every part of me reacts instantly, heat pooling in my stomach as goosebumps break out on my skin.

"Look at you," he whispers, his voice almost a growl. "I can feel every inch of you on edge for me."

"Heath, you can't do this here," I gasp, trying to stay focused as I glance nervously toward the glass walls of my office.

He tilts his head, almost as if he's savoring my discomfort. "No, no," he says, shaking his head. "I wouldn't let your colleagues have the pleasure. But there is one thing I really like about this office."

"What's that?" I ask, my voice barely a whisper, knowing full well what's coming next.

He grins, and it's a smile that sends a chill down my spine. He steps closer, his hand landing gently around my throat as he pushes me back toward my desk. My chair hits the ground with a thud, and before I can process what's happening, Heath is kneeling beneath my desk, his body hidden from view. He pulls my rolling chair closer, his face aligned with my lap.

"The meal service," he murmurs, his voice hushed, but loaded with dark humor.

GISELE

"Heath!" I protested, slapping a hand on the top of his head to push at him. He easily resisted and kissed his way up the inside of my thigh, lifting my dress as he went and gripping me tight in place.

"Oh God, please!" Then, a sharp pain blisters through my center. I jerk my head down to find him fucking biting me, his teeth clamping around my clit.

"What did I tell you?" he snarls.

"I'm sorry," I whimper. "I'm sorry."

"What do you say?"

"Heath," I breathe. "Heath." His teeth loosen, and his tongue laps up the pain.

His name falls from my lips once more as my eyes roll to the back of my head.

"Mmm," he moans. "I know I make you feel good, baby, but everyone outside can see you. Least you can do is pretend to have it together."

My head snaps up once again, and then down to him. He looks up at me with a shit-eating grin. Or...a pussy-eating grin. Fucking fuck, I am so fucked.

I pick up a pen from my desk and pretend to edit a proposal in case anyone walks by, looking for superfluous commas and extra spaces. But I can't focus on shit. My vision is blurring, every inch of my body tingling. Two of Heath's fingers slip into me easily, and the sound of my own cunt resonate in the air. I am embarrassingly wet, my legs trembling.

As I look down at the paper in front of me, two knocks sound at the door. I don't look up. Can't.

"Fuck, Heath," I whisper at the document. "Someone's at the door."

"Good," he says, lapping at my center still. "Let them in."

**8**

**CHAPTER 8**

G ISELE

"No, I can't. I can't. I'm gonna—Ouch! Fuck!" I look down to find his teeth clamped around my clit once again, his smile in place.

"Let. Them. In. And don't you make a fucking sound. Only I get to hear you." Two more knocks at the door. I burry my lips in my teeth, taking a deep breath and trying to hold in the orgasm that is creeping up fast. Lifting my face to the door, I smile falsely. It is Dylan. He shrugs at me through the glass as if to ask where Heath has gone off to, and I shake my head innocently. I hope he would take that as -- Nothing to worry about. I have it handled.

But, instead, he enters. Shit.

"Where'd our new client run off to?" he asks, slinking through the door of my office. "Bathroom," I blurt as Heath's fingers curls up to my G-spot, his tongue circling my clit. "Hm." Dylan squints his eyes at me. "You okay? You seem a little tense." I force a giggle, about to fucking explode. "Fine, yeah. Fine." Dyl an turns to the bookshelf on the left side of my office, satisfied with my answer. Running his eyes over the titles, he says, "I would've much rather taken our meeting than have you stuck here with a client, but I suppose I can push my three o'clock back."The ministrations on my pussy stops in an instant, and I catch my breath. Never have I been so glad to have my pleasure cut right before an orgasm. I glance down between my legs. Heath shakes his head back and forth slowly."I can't." I look back up at Dylan, who turns again to face me, disappointment taking his features. "I have a virtual meeting," I lie, and Heath's lips reach me once again. I use my one hand to grab hair at his forehead and pull his head back to make him spare me from this torture, but his lips once again fall back on my pussy.I claw at the desk in an attempt to get a hold of myself, his attention on my pussy becoming more desperate. He likes my answer. I can tell he is rewarding me. Nothing can stop him now that he is happy with me.Dylan sighs and turns back towards the books, pulling an encyclopedia from the shelf and letting it flop open in his palm. My hips began grinding into Heath's face desperately, his free hand digging into my thigh.

I want to scream his name. I want to go absolutely fucking wild for him. At this moment, I can't care less how fucked up it all is. It feels better than anything I've ever felt before. I need to come for him. Need him to taste it all.

My pussy tightens as his fingers slips in and out, my shaky legs squeezing his shoulders. I take Dylan's focus on the book pages as an opportunity to slap a hand over my mouth and scream silently into my palm, shaking and shuddering all over my seat with a mind-numbing orgasm. It's not that Dylan has never seen me come before, though it is infrequent. But, obviously, this is different. And much better. Much, much bette r.Heath's tongue doesn't stop moving around my sensitive clit after I finish, and he is quickly driving me right into overstimulation. I have a feeling that is very intentional and another feeling he'd not be stopping any time soon. I kick at his side with my heel, silently begging him to stop, but he only claw into me harder, swirling his tongue, soaking everything between my legs."Well," Dylan says, slapping the book shut. "I imagine our friend will be back soon. I'll leave you to it." He slides the book back into its spot and steps out the door with a soft smile.The second the door shuts behind him, I let out a breath, and then a whimper, and then a straight-up squeal."Heath, stop!" I whine, grinding my hips into his face."Say it like you mean it and I will," he groans.Oh, fuck.

I grab his head with two hands and slide right out of my seat like goo, falling onto the floor in front of him and taking his mouth in mine. He crashes over me like a wave, devouring me, teeth and tongue, his lips smearing over mine with intense hu nger."Aw, baby!" he exclaims, lifting his head for only a second. "Our first kiss!""Shut the fuck up, Heath, and fuck me right now," I order as he press me into the floor."Yes, of course, my sweet gift," he obliges desperately, his expression becoming quite serious.I lie back on the rug behind my desk as Heath undo his suit pants and whips his cock out. Lifting a hand in the air, I motion him to stop, staring at it as I jerk backward."What the hell is that?" I ask. Is this man a half-horse?

He looks down at his enormous dick, then back at my face. "It's yours." Heath's hands wrap around my hips, and he drags me underneath him, placing his tip at my entrance. "It's yours," he repeated, pushing into me without hesitation.My eyes flutter shut, my body arching into the floor of my office as I whimper. No one can save me in this moment. I'm officially gone. With the way his cock feels inside of me, I would've let him do quite literally whatever he wants.He pushes deeper, stretching me perfectly as I feel every inch of him sliding in and out. I moan loudly, and he slaps a hand over my lips. Fuck, it smells like me."You're such a good girl, you know that?" he murmurs, squeezing my cheeks and jerking my face to look up at him as he fucks me. He leans down in my ear, his thrusts coming harder and faster as I scream into his hand. "My good girl. Only mine."

HEATH

I sit in my office, alone, the clock ticking by in a way that only deepens the restlessness inside me. It's been hours since Gisele pushed me out, but I can still taste her on my lips. I close my eyes and let the memory flood me, the warmth of her mouth, the soft pressure of her body against mine. That moment in her office, on the floor, is etched into my mind, and I know I'll never forget it. I don't want to.

But more than the memory, it's the future I'm obsessed with. Her. She will be mine. Forever.

I can't stop the thoughts from spiraling—how it will feel when she's always by my side, how we'll carve out a life together. How her name would sound like with my last name. Gisele Steinfeld. Fuck, I can't wait for that day to come. I need it.

I check my email, hoping for some distraction, but it's the same as before. Dylan's email is still sitting unanswered in my inbox, the CEO's response nowhere to be found. I don't care about work right now, though. Not really. My mind keeps drifting back to Gisele, to the way she looked at me when she said goodbye. That fire in her eyes, it's something I want to see every day.

Max is the next logical choice. I step out of my office and cross the hall to his. He's slouched in the corner, looking as un-bothered as always, his eyes heavy with boredom. He doesn't move when I enter. I can tell he's deep in his own thoughts. Whatever. I don't need him to talk to me right now. I check my watch—4:30 p.m.

Only one more hour, I tell myself. One more hour and she'll be home from work.

I leave the organization and make my way to my bike, shoving my head into my black helmet. Whipping around the building and down the street, I ride to my apartment for the first time in a few days.

I've been so focused on Gisele. The organization is closer to her house, so I've been staying there. Opening the door to my place, I realize it is the first time I've been in here since meeting her, and it makes my skin crawl. It is so clean and modern. So high-end. My heart twists thinking that Gisele lives with the roaches while I am here.

She should be here, too, enjoying a little luxury. I'll bring her here. Yes. She will live here.

I slunk to my walk-in closet and eat up another twenty minutes of waiting time by clearing out half my drawers and shelves, pushing my clothes in tight to make space for my girl. My heart warms as I back up and review my work. So many clean, empty shelves for her to fill. I pull out my phone to call her. She picks up after the second ring.

**9**

CHAPTER 9

H EATH

I pull my phone out, dialing her number before I can second-guess myself. She answers after two rings, her voice clipped.

"Heath? I can't talk right now."

"Then why did you pick up, little Gisele?" I drag a finger lazily across the row of shirts hanging in front of me, a grin tugging at my lips.

There's a sharp click on the other end, the sound of her teeth clashing. I can practically hear her rolling her eyes. My grin widens, the tension in the air between us already palpable.

"You fucked up my carpet," she says, a mix of irritation and amusement in her voice.

I chuckle, leaning against the closet frame, stretching out my legs. "Mmm," I groan. "Don't remind me."

"I'm serious! I don't know what the hell to tell the cleaning people. I can still see the mark."

I shake my head, amusement lacing my words. "That wasn't me, baby. I made sure to come inside of you. Promise."

Her growl on the other end makes my pulse quicken. Damn, she sounds too fucking sexy when she's annoyed. "Goodbye, Heath," she snaps, her voice sharp as she cuts the call.

"Wait!" I call after her. "Don't go." But she is already gone.

My smile falls to a whine. Whatever. It is practically 5:15 anyway. By the time I make it to hers, she'd be home. Fucking finally.

I grab a few things from my kitchen, tossing them into a plastic bag which I then shove in the compartment of my bike before driving off.

I have to grip the railing just to make sure I didn't fall to my fucking death as I trudge up the worn stairs to Gisele's apartment. When I pick the lock and enter through her front door, she is sitting on her couch with a glass of wine in hand.

"Relaxing already, pretty girl? "Her head whips around to look at my unmasked face, and she jumps out of her seat, squealing.

"Heath!"

"And already screaming my name? "She empties the last sip of her wine down her throat and slams the lip of the glass on her coffee table, shattering the cup. Holding it by the intact stem, she backs into the far corner of the living room, jags glass edges pointed at me.

My joy is an explosion. What a smart girl. I am glad she knows how to react quickly if an intruder ever come after her, what with the shampoo bottle the other night and now the wine glass.

She is so fucking clever and so fucking strong. I admire that about her.

"You can't keep coming here," she asserts.

I sigh and leave the items I've brought on the kitchen counter. My stubborn girl. Always playing this game with me, as if we don't end up in the same place each and every time; with her moaning my name.

"I brought food," I say casually, reaching into the plastic bag and pulling out a container of dried pasta from my freezer and a jar of sauce from my fridge.

I hold each of them up in my hands. "I made them myself. Thought we could watch a movie."

"Oh, Heath, you are so fucking off your rocker!" Her hand is shaking as she holds out her improvised weapon, perhaps from anger. I doubt it is fear. No, she looks far more angry. Definitely frustrated.

"Am not!" I tease, placing the food down on the counter and approaching her with a smile. "Just because I'm a little...diffe rent doesn't mean I'm any less human, baby." I tilt my head to the side, now only afoot away from her.

"Different?!" she grits as I step closer to the shards in her hand. "There is something missing up there!" She nudges her chin to my face, indicating she is referring to my head.

Silly. My head is perfectly fine. "Brains are funny, Gis. No two are the same. While yours excels incorporate America, mine excels at making you wet."

She growls, pounding an irritated fist at her side. "Neither is better than the other. We are simply different."

I pull my sweatshirt off in one smooth motion, my T-shirt coming off with it. I see her eyes widen, hunger flashing in her gaze. It's the same look she gave me before. She can't resist, and neither can I.

I step closer, my chest nearly touching hers now, my hands braced against the wall behind her. I trap her in place, my body pressing against the sharp edges of the glass she holds. The cool touch of the shards against my skin sends a rush of sensation through me, and I groan, allowing myself to sink further, to let her feel the danger of it.

"Ahh," I hiss as the glass breaks my skin, blood starting to bead along the cut. It stings, but I don't care. Not when she's here, not when she's this close.

She stands frozen, her breath shallow, her eyes locked on me. She's not running, not even trying to get away. Instead, she watches me like I'm some kind of puzzle, something she's trying to figure out. I like that.

"You know that saying?" I whisper, my voice low, painful. "Don't judge a fish by its ability to climb a tree, or whatever."

She doesn't say anything, but her attention never leaves me. The tension in the room thickens, and I can feel the pull between us, the magnetic force that neither of us can resist.

"Same goes for me, baby," I say, my voice low, laced with something dangerous. "Don't judge me by my ability to follow rules. I simply don't do that. Neither my dad followed rules, nor my mother. I'm really good at some other things. Like fucking you, for example."

I pause, letting the words sink in, before adding, "And really bad at others. Like..."

"Boundaries?" She slams the glass into my chest, her eyes narrowing on the cuts, her stare a fire that burns through me.

"Like staying away from you," I finish, my voice just above a whisper, thick with the truth.

She doesn't hesitate. "I hope you get smaller shards lodged in your skin, you fucking psycho." Her words cut as deep as any glass, and before I can react, she rips it from my body and hurls it to the ground, the crash sharp and cold like the ice in her veins.

She presses her hands to my chest, shoving me hard. She fucking shoves me. Again.

Bad girl.

I snap, grabbing her by the back of the head, pulling her close, my grip fierce. "Do not ever do that again."

But she does. She pushes me again. And the rage—it's a firestorm, boiling up from the depths of my gut, filling my chest, consuming me. I grab her head with both hands, forcing her face toward mine. "I'm going to make you fucking sing for me," I growl.

"You're going to leave me the fuck alone!" she screams, her defiance burning bright.

I block her knee with a hand, grinning, because I know what's coming. Predictable. Her knee slams into me, and I laugh. I fucking laugh.

"Why would I do that?" I ask, voice dripping with amusement. I tilt my head, grinning wide, locking eyes with her gray ones. "Don't pretend you're not just as desperate as I am, little Gisele."

She pushes me again, but I hold her tight, relentless. "I absolutely am not!"

I lean in, my forehead brushing against hers. "You absolutely are."

Frustration is written all over her face, her chest heaving with the struggle to keep it together. I can see the moment when she cracks, when she almost gives in to the temptation of my lips, but instead, she does something unexpected.

She drops her hand to my chest, trying to stop the flow of blood. She's a wild girl, a dangerous one.

Her pout deepens as she slides over me, and I can feel the shiver run through me as she pushes her hand against my chest. She quickly climbs up my body, her hands gripping my shoulders, and just when I think she'll kiss me, she doesn't. She drags her lips to mine, and I bite down on them, tasting her, feeling the heat radiate between us.

"See, baby?" I whisper, pressing my tongue into her mouth, showing her how much I know. "Just like me."

Lucky man. I'm a fucking lucky man. She tastes like wine, and everything I've ever wanted. My future.

We lose ourselves in each other, our bodies fighting to taste every inch, every molecule of the other. I carry her behind the couch, throwing her down, making sure she's got enough support beneath her head. Sweatpants are torn off in a rush, and the ecstasy that floods me is immediate, intense, as I sink into her, claiming her, filling every void.

It's everything. It's more than everything. It's what we both need.

**10**

***

## CHAPTER 10

G isele

I scream into the couch pillow beneath me as Heath fucks me hard and fast. The position is absolutely destroying me. I can't even squirm. My feet hardly hit the floor and my body is draped over the couch like a throw, my legs stretching down painfully.

His moans fill my ears, and there is something so fucking intoxicating about hearing just how much he is enjoying himself. How much he is enjoying me.

God, his cock is fucking enormous, and I am sore. So, so sore, but so, so good. I need a hot bath. No, I need a fucking baptism at this point.

A large hand grabs the back of my head, pulling my hair until my neck burned from bending in half. I yelp as Heath continues to take me as he please.

Peering to the side at the long mirror on my living room wall, I catch a glimpse of him. He is wearing trousers tonight, black ones, and his black boots. His pants sit undone just under his hips which smack hard against my ass, and his arms and torso are fully bare, save the tattoos that stretch around his skin.

I watch him slam into me rhythmically, his head tilting back, his lips parted, his abs flexing and his arms tensing. He looks incredible.

"Heath, yo-huh." Fuck, I can't even speak, but I need to let this man know he looks like a fucking painting. There is something he does to me that I just can't figure out. It's like he turns on my pussy and turns off my brain, making me bend to his will.

He wraps his arms around me and pulls me into his front, crushing me in a hug. My spine arched, his cock hitting me deeper this way and forcing me to shriek.

"Tell me," he whispers in my ear, grabbing my face with one hand and kissing the corner of my mouth from behind.

"I wu-ah... I wanted t-to..."

He slows down his movements for a moment, settling deep inside of me and hugging me tight until I get my word in.

"I wanted to tell you that you look beautiful," I rush out.

He catches my gaze in our reflection in the mirror. If I was worried before that Heath has a few screws loose, I was completely positive when I see his expression change. His mouth stretches, his teeth two bright, straight lines as he grins like a depraved man. So...like himself.

He immediately forces my head down to the couch, his fingers in my hair, as he fucks me faster and slaps my butt with his free hand. I yelp at the stinging contact.

"See, my sweet gift? I knew you'd fucking come around." He slaps me again, harder this time, my skin burning twice as hot. "Fuck, you look so pretty taking my cock." Again, his palm hit me, and I wonder if I could bleed from a slap so hard. "Tell me how much you love it. Tell me how fucking good you feel."

I practically sob as he pulls my head back by way of my hair, my neck bending again, making it hard to breathe. "I love it," I choke.

He slaps my butt once more. "Who's my good girl?"

"I'm your good girl," I cry, my dignity be damned.

He groans, holding my head with two hands to brace me as he slams into my pussy impossibly fast. His movements force me to break, and I clamp around him like a fucking vise as he releases a whimper of his own, his hips pressing inward, his hot cum filling me up.

Heath don't stop watching me while I try to shower. He insists I leave the curtain open as he lays his dick in the sink, rinsing it under the stream from the faucet. He buries his teeth in his bottom lip, watching me clean off what we've just done in the living room. He looks so annoyingly giddy.

After I finish up, he wraps me in a towel before zipping up his pants and leaving me to get dressed. I pull on my black sweatpants-sweatshirt combo and make my way out to the kitchen. When I enter, he's standing casually at the stove in front of one of my pots, waiting for water to boil.

What the actual fuck? He's fucking cooking.

The fucker has made himself so at home here, I wonder if he even has a place to stay. Maybe he's trying to squat or something. What kind of intruder shows up with food and then starts cooking?

When Heath is close to me, my brain loses all sensibility. My body begs for him, and I can't help myself.

But every time I come, there's a short moment of clarity before he works me back up again, during which I question all my life choices. This is one of those moments.

I can't believe I let him fuck me again. Can't believe I let him be here without calling the fucking cops. When will this end? Am I ever going to get my head on straight? I shake off the thought and reach under the kitchen counter for the dustpan to pick up my little wine glass fiasco.

"I already picked it up," he says over his shoulder, dumping a plastic container of pasta into the boiling pot. "Ran my bare feet over the floor to make sure there were no little shards, too."

I look down at his feet, which are, in fact, bare. He wriggles his giant toes at me.

Seriously, though. Are criminals always this fucking boyish? I straighten myself up, abandoning my movements to fetch the dustpan, and approach him, crossing my arms and thumping my hip against the counter.

"Did you really make that?" I mumble. The guy is here and, obviously, there's nothing I can do about it. Might as well make conversation with him.

He nods his head proudly, turning to look at me. "I like to cook." I arch an eyebrow. I've never thought to ask a thief what his hobbies are. "What do you like to do?"

"Shouldn't you already know that?" I sneer. He tilts his head like he doesn't understand. "Aren't you some kind of stalker? Don't you know everything?"

He dons a thoughtful look and shrugs his shoulders. "I mean... I know your name is Gisele Campbell, born in New York City. Your parents are happily living their marriage life in Mont-clair. You have an elder brother named Archie who recently graduated and started working in finance. His girlfriend is the daughter of a popular singer. I forgot his name-"

"What?" I blurt out, "He has a girlfriend?"

He nods, "You didn't know? They recently started dating. No trace in media, but jeez, he should have at least told you."

"Okay, okay. I will ask him about it later" I mumble, not wanting to hear another word about my family from an intruder. He knows too much. I hold up a hand in his direction, and his shoulders fall.

"Gisele, I just want to know what you like to do," he says innocently, blinking twice.

"Drink wine," I bite, grabbing a new glass from the cabinet. "And masturbate."

His innocent stare melts into a wild smile, and he laughs. "You're very funny, you know. You're funny in a way that makes me think you don't mean to be funny."

I roll my eyes. "That's because you're delusional, Heath. I bet everything is hilarious when you're so far 'round the bend."

"It is." He nods with a soft grin. "I bet everything is sad when you're so stagnant in life."

I scoff as I turn toward the kitchen island to fetch an open bottle of wine. "Fuck you, Heath."

"Again?"

"No—"

In an instant, he spins me around and kisses me, pressing my back into the island. By the look on his face as he does so, I know he's joking; that he isn't really such an idiot to think I actually want to fuck him again.

It's honestly a bit of a relief that he recognizes that. So, the guy has some lucidity. And god, he's fucking good at kissing.

"Heath," I whisper as his kisses get more passionate, more wet.

He ignores my attempt to get him to stop and bites into me deeper still, palming my hips in his hands and squeezing me hard. Fuck, there's no way I can stop him and no way I actually want to. What the fuck is wrong with me?

I reach up to grab his silky, black hair in both hands and tug on it.

He groans and spins me around so my back hits his front. I stare at the pot of boiling water, now filled with slowly unfurling noodles. He grabs a wooden spoon from the counter and gives the food a single twirl.

"I don't want to get distracted," he says, placing the spoon down and reaching both arms around me to open the jar of sauce. He dumps it in a smaller pot on the burner next to the pasta. "I want you to eat well, but it'll come out like shit if I leave it here too long while I fuck you again."

# 11

## CHAPTER 11

G ISELE

"Pity," I say, shrugging a shoulder.

He laughs at that, his chest vibrating at the back of my head, before picking the wooden spoon back up and swirling it through the sauce. With his free hand, he reaches into my pants.

"Heath!" I squeal, leaning forward in shock but he catches me just before my face hit the hot stove.

"I can do both," he says, his hand again starts stirring the food with one hand and my pussy with the other.

Oh, fuck, why is this so hot?

I fall backward into his naked chest, my hands holding his bare biceps as I moan, watching him cook, then digging my forehead into his upper arm, then simply letting my head fall back and my eyes shut.

He remains focused on his work until I come and the pasta finished cooking. Weird, weird, weird fucking man. The weirdest.

Heath pulls his hand from my pants, hooking his arm around my neck as he leans forward to suck his fingers over my shoulder. Releasing the tips with a smack, he moans with pleasure and undo his hold around me.

"Go sit on the couch, my sweet gift."

He is always calling me that.

The pasta tastes good. Really, really good. It's cooked just right, and the sauce? Incredible.

"How's it, baby?" Heath asks, clearing the plates from the table before plopping down beside me again.

"Fine." I cross my arms, my eyes fixed on the TV screen as he pours us both another glass of wine.

Sitting here with Heath, it's strangely normal. As if he's my boyfriend, just here for dinner and a movie. I hate myself for not feeling more unsettled about it.

Even though I'm not uncomfortable, I'm fully aware that I should be working on my pitch for next week. But in the last two days? I've spent exactly zero minutes on it at home. How could I? I'm being stalked, and fucked, by a hot robber.

Robber. Is he really a robber. He never minds me when I call him that.

He said his parents didn't follow rules either. Were they robbers too?

I grab my notebook from the coffee table, pushing aside the fact that Heath is sitting right next to me. If he shows up at my place randomly, he'll have to deal with the fact that I've got things to do.

I half expect him to say something about it, but he doesn't. Instead, he shifts closer, leaning back against the couch and peering down at my notebook. His gaze follows me as I try to piece together a coherent thought.

"What're you doing?" he asks, nuzzling his face into my neck.

"You're like an annoying little puppy, you know that?"

"Mmm." He presses a soft kiss to my shoulder. "Maybe I spend too much time around dogs."

"Dogs?" I glance at him, pausing my writing for a second.

"I work with a lot of dogs. Animals, really."

"Ah, right." I scoff, my shoulders shaking slightly from the laugh he's managed to pull from me. "I can't imagine your crime colleagues being exactly civil."

"Silly girl," he whispers.

I sigh, leaning into him reluctantly. What else can I do?

"I've got a pitch next week."

"A pitch?"

I nod. "It's a big one. I should've been working on it when you decided to show up. I have to make filing cabinets sound interesting. Can you believe that?"

He sits up straighter, a thoughtful look crossing his face. After a moment, he speaks. "I think it's fitting." He looks at me, an eyebrow arched. "Filing cabinets keep your documents safe and organized. Sell that."

I roll my eyes. Is that the best he's got? It's the same tired advice I've heard a thousand times. "You're not selling a pen; you're selling a handwritten note to your family." "You're not selling plates; you're selling a romantic dinner with your partner." Blah. Blah. Blah.

I ignore him and go back to my notes.

"What if..." He leans in, grabbing me by the waist and pulling me across his lap, making me lay face-up against him. "A woman has this really important document..." He leans in close, his lips brushing my neck. "And a thief—a super hot one, with a huge cock—breaks into her office and just tears the whole thing up."

"Seems a little taboo," I say, raising an eyebrow.

"Good. People will talk about it." He lifts a finger, the smile spreading across his face. "He sees the filing cabinet, how dull it looks, and decides it's not worth his time. He takes everything else. Her document? Safe."

I snort. "From a real thief's perspective, would you really steal from a filing cabinet?"

"In case I was a real thief, I wouldn't even steal the queen's jewels if you were there, my gift. I'd be too busy staring into your pretty eyes."

"I'm not your gift. I'm your victim." I make sure he remembers that.

"Victim. A person who's harmed or in danger," he whispers, trailing his lips up my neck, then over my jaw. "You didn't seem so much like a victim when you were being my good, little girl."

God, I can't help it. I drop the notebook onto the coffee table and throw my arms around his neck, pulling him down to kiss me.

"You taste like pasta sauce," he murmurs against my lips, his grin widening.

I'm about to crack a joke—"Pasta sauce you made me eat"—when I freeze. If he'd been so fucking generous with my milk, what the hell has he put in the sauce? I shove him off me and scramble into the corner of the couch.

"What the hell did you put in the sauce?"

That grin of his just widens. He sits back on the couch, never breaking eye contact, casually grabbing his crotch as if it's no big deal.

"Nothing you haven't eaten before, baby."

"Oh, Heath!" I grab a couch pillow and throw it at him. "I'm going to fucking kill you!"

He reaches for the pillow to throw it back, but I dodge it easily, jumping to my feet. He lunges for me, but I slip away, sprinting toward the bedroom.

It's a dumb idea, I know. The place is tiny—hardly 600 square feet—and I've only got a few seconds.

I dive into the bedroom, trying to use the bed as a barrier between us. He's after me immediately, grinning like a maniac.

"You can't keep doing this, Heath!" I squeal, backing up.

"What?" he asks innocently. "I just said it's nothing you haven't eaten before." He's fast—so fast—that before I can get around the bed, he's already on the other side, moving in to grab me.

I bolt, trying to make it to the door, but he catches my ankle and slams me back onto the mattress.

"You've eaten olive oil, haven't you? Salt?" His hands grip my body, pulling me towards him, his weight pinning me down. There's no escaping it, and honestly, I'm not sure I even want to anymore.

"You didn't come in the sauce?" I ask, breathless.

He tilts his head back and laughs. I can't help but stare at the way his shoulders flex, the tattoos across his chest and arms shifting.

"No, silly girl!" He lets out a wicked laugh, but then his expression shifts. His eyes darken slightly. "But since you're begging for my cum..."

The bastard lets go of me and drops me onto the floor like I'm nothing. I try to scramble, but he's already on top of me, straddling my body.

With his knees trapping my arms beneath him, he unzips his pants. His cock springs free, right in front of my face.

"If you don't want it, don't open your mouth," he says with wide eyes, one hand gripping the top of my head by way of my hair.

"Funny you'd give me the choice after forcing your way into my apartment."

He grips my hair tighter, those baby blues burning with icy fire. "Decision made, then. And I have never done anything you didn't want. You can't honestly tell me that's not true."

Before I can answer, he fills my mouth with his cock, thrusting into me hard. The back of my throat burns, my jaw stretching, my eyes springing leaks almost instantaneously. I stare up at him, at the H, at his tattoos, and the way his eyes look in the dim light of my room. The shadows from the light of the living room just outside the door dance on his abs, highlighting every peak and contrasting every canyon. His blue eyes glimmer, his teeth peeking out from between those perfect fucking lips.

He looks way too fucking pretty. God, I just fucking hate it.

I wonder if this is really any worse than meeting assholes on dating apps. I mean, at least this guy can fuck me right. And he seems to care about me. Too much.

But, hell, the guys I'd been going on dates with for the better part of my twenties are straight-up assholes. Guys my age are absolute—

Wait a second...

I try to scream, to make noise so he'd stop.

He giggles and pulls out. "That tickles, baby."

"How old are you?" I ask, my lungs gasping for air. I assume he is early to mid twenties but... I don't know. I guess I am curious.

He cocks his head. "Twenty-four."

"I'm twenty-three" I choke.

He smiles. "I know."

I return to thinking about the guys I'd dated during the last decade or so. Sure, they all pretended to be nice, but I know well enough they were sending around girls' nudes to each other and getting chicks too drunk to function just so they could take them home and fuck them.

I am not sure I've ever met a guy who don't do those things. But, I don't know. Heath doesn't really seem like the type. He kind of seems like if he wants to fuck someone, he'd just...do it. No alcohol. No secret games.

"You're not paying attention," he says. "Eyes on me. Up here"

**12**

—  •  —

## CHAPTER 12

G ISELE

Heath spends the night at my place. Like, actually in my bed. And the weirdest part? He drives me to work this morning on his terrifying bike, insists I wear his helmet, and promises he'll buy another one so we can both be safe next time.

Of everything—every bit of stalking, all the pressure to hook up with him—the weirdest and most disturbing thing he's done so far is act like a normal boyfriend. A normal guy doing normal things. And honestly? I'm not really disturbed by it at all. In fact, I kind of... like it. I've never been the type to win popularity contests.

People take too much effort. I don't want to fake conversations, remind myself to ask them questions, and try hard to socialize the "right" way.But Heath? He's something else entirely.Being around him is terrifying. Orgasmic. Confusing. Strange. But it's never boring. I never have to force myself to interact. I can be dripping wet and naked, makeup smeared all over my face, or lounging in my sweatpants after a shitty day—and he still looks at me like I'm the greatest thing to walk the earth.

Sure, he doesn't actually know me—hell, he doesn't know anything about me—but I can't pretend I hate the validation. Or the sex. We reach the office building, and Heath follows me up to my floor. He's not in his usual suit today, which leaves me wondering how we're going to explain this if anyone notices us. Walking in with a "client" dressed in a casual black sweatshirt? Definitely not a great look. But I'm sure Heath will come up with some excuse.

The guy's good at talking his way out of things.Dylan and Carly are standing at the reception desk when Heath and I step out of the elevator. Dylan's always flirting with Carly. It's nothing new. I don't care. Talking to Carly is like talking to cotton candy—she's sweet, but there's nothing there. Dylan probably likes that in a hit-it-and-quit-it kind of way. Fine by me. As far as I'm concerned, he can do whatever he wants, as long as I get a raise at the end of the fiscal year for all the... services I've been providing.

Dylan perks up the second he sees Heath behind me. For a moment, I catch a flicker of worry in his eyes, but it's gone in an instant, replaced by that slimy, salesy grin of his."Mr. Steinfeld! Couldn't stay away from her, huh?" Dylan chuckles, but there's a definite edge to his voice.Heath leans forward, hands in his pockets, letting his jaw drop as he lets out an exaggerated, completely fake laugh. He looks like a fucking madman. It's... hot. Then he shakes Dylan's hand, leans on the reception desk, and winks at Carly.

He's doing that to mess with Dylan, I'm sure—since he's clearly trying to get Carly's attention. I won't lie though, it makes me the tiniest bit jealous."I saw Miss Campbell on the street and had to walk her to her building. How lucky am I?" Heath says, his voice dripping with fake sweetness."The luckiest!" Dylan replies, laying a hand on his chest as if he's a romantic lead in some shitty drama. "Thanks for returning her to us."Heath's eyes catch mine, and he raises an eyebrow, silently asking, Really? This fucking guy? I bite my lip to stop myself from smiling."I don't know what we'd do without Miss Campbell, here," Dylan continues, sliding his hand a little too low on my back.Heath doesn't miss a beat.

He freezes for a second, staring at Dylan's hand on my body, his face blank. Then, he snaps back to the moment, offering another fake laugh. "Okay, you three," he says, acting like we're all best pals. "I'll leave you to it. I'll be in touch." His eyes lock on mine again—those piercing, glacial blues—and he pulls his phone out of his pocket, waving it in the air as if to remind me he'll be listening.

HEATH

I bolt toward the elevator before things get weird. Not that I think Dylan's a real threat, but Gisele is still playing games. She's still pretending like we're not together, like she's not mine. Once she fully admits it, I won't need to worry. For now, I've still got to deal with her being in denial, and yeah, it makes me insecure.

Before I even make it halfway to the street, I've already got my earbuds in. I lean against the wooden wall of the elevator, close my eyes, and turn the volume up, listening as best as I can. The sound's muffled. Her phone's probably still in her bag."I think our new client has a crush on you," Dylan says."Funny," Heath scoffs. I hear a rustle, her heels clicking as she moves.

Good girl, I think. Keep it short. Walk away."And what do you think of him?" Dylan's following her now. "Dylan Jones, are you asking if I have a crush?"A crush? What the hell does he mean by that? I've been inside her body at least three times, and I don't need a fucking dictionary to know how far we've gone. I find the use of the word crush offensive."I just think he's a little off. Don't you? Something crazy in his eyes like he wants to eat us all with a fork and knife," Gisele says.

Only you, babygirl. Dylan's probably a flavorless, after-shave-scented bore."He's..." I can hear her pause, thinking of what to say next. "Quirky. Very good at his job, though. I'll give him that.""What does he do, anyway?" Dylan asks. His voice sounds small, nervous. Another pause."Home security."I can practically hear her smirking now, like she knows I'm listening.

Like she's messing with me behind her lame boss' back.F uck, I have the best girlfriend.For now.Soon enough, she'll be Gisele Steinfeld, and god, I love how that sounds.Dylan and

Gisele finish their casual chat, but by now, I don't care. He leaves her alone, and after a beat of silence, she giggles."I think he's onto you." I smile wide, pull out my phone, and shoot her a quick text: Good.I take out my earbuds and slip my helmet on, feeling the faint scent of her shampoo on it. It almost drives me insane. Fuck, I want her every second of every day.I mount my bike and head to the organization.

**13**

CHAPTER 13

H EATH

When I arrive, Neil and other men are nowhere to be found, and Max is grumpy as hell. He's still slouched in his usual corner, lethargic and sick as ever. The sight tugs at my heart.

I really don't want him to die. He has a severe bone tumor in his left leg, which is why he spends so much time sitting around instead of joining us on jobs. He went through surgery too, but it didn't help him much. He's lost the use of his leg and spends most of his time sulking.

"Hey boss" I say, sitting next to him. "How you been?"

He grunts in response.

"Yep." I pat his back, trying to be reassuring. "Don't worry. You'll be fine soon."

"Mr. Steinfeld." I turn and see Eva standing in the doorway. Had she always been this plain, or is it just that Gisele makes everything else look dull by comparison?

"Eva, please. Call me Heath." I've told her a hundred times.

Mr. Steinfeld is for my father. Heath is for those closest to me. And she, Eva, is daughter of my father's friend, Leo.

"Heath. My apologies."

She tries too hard to be polite. It annoys me, but she's not all bad.

I flop into the chair behind my desk and kick my boots up onto the surface, staring around the office that used to be my father's. Now he has handled it to me. I'm not that well as compared to how he was when he was my age, but I try to be like him. He had to go through this when he was young, without any support.

I sigh, things are easier when he is there to support me, with his big team who is enjoying life as if they have retired. Though, they often come around whenever I need them.

The last few months have been rough at work, I got scolded by father for taking some stupid decisions. Plus, my mom and dad, both would kill me if they knew what I'm doing here with Gisele. They'd only hear the "breaking into the house of a poor girl and fucking her" part.

Now that I think of it, I can't wait to have Gisele meeting my mom and sister. I can maybe make some changes into the story which pleases them.

I sigh and refocus, opening my laptop to check Dylan's inbox. The guy seems to be missing a lot of important stuff. But I don't care. The only thing I'm really looking for is a new message from Mark Evans, CEO. And I finally find it. Fucking finally.

Dylan,While I appreciate your passion for Miss Campbell's accomplishments, I'm afraid we don't have the facilities to accommodate your request. Given her recent pay raise in January, we've done all we can to ensure Miss Campbell is compensated for her hard work and dedication. I understand she's special to you, but as you know, my hands are tied.—Mark

A recent pay raise in January? That can't be right. My Gisele is ambitious, not selfish. I quickly scramble to the financial records, pulling up the bill processing platform to dig into her payments.

The deposits are automatic, just as I expected, but there are no changes—no increase in amount, no change in method. Nothing has changed in the last two years since she took the position.

Fuck, the numbers on her statements are low. I thought for sure she'd be making a lot more, especially with that fancy office they've got her in.

What the hell is going on?

I keep checking every record, scrutinizing every detail for any hint of discrepancies, all while side-eyeing the growing pile of papers stacked on the corner of my desk—my own work, waiting for me.

Shit.

Between figuring out Gisele's financials and sorting through the mess of the organization's accounts, it's going to be a long fucking night.

GISELE

I sit on the couch, showered and comfortable after work, when my phone chimes. A text from Unknown. It's probably Heath. I still haven't even bothered to save his number.

Unknown: I can't make it tonight, baby :(

As if I'd fucking invited him in the first place.

Unknown: I've been neglecting my work for you, and it's caught up to me.

Me: Off to rob more apartments and find more girls in the shower?

Unknown: Funny.

Unknown: I'll be in the office late.

Unknown: [Photo]

I look at the photo he sends—an oddly normal shot of a stack of paperwork on a standard desk. Isn't he a robber? A thief? Does he have... a day job?

Me: What do you do for work?

The curiosity claws at me. This guy is a fucking mystery, and every time I think I'm starting to get a handle on him, he throws another curveball.

Unknown: I told you. I work with animals.

Ah, right. He works with criminals and lowlifes. I got that much. But... stacks of paperwork?

Me: Fine, then. Be vague.

Me: Have a good night.

Unknown: No touching yourself without me.

Unknown: I'll be watching.

Wait a minute...

Me: Watching?! I thought you were just listening sometimes...

Me: Heath...

Me: Heath! Answer me!

Unknown: I have a lot of work, my pretty gift. Enjoy your night off :)

I growl, throwing my phone down on the couch, then hold up both middle fingers in the air, just in case he's got cameras or something weird like that. Wouldn't put it past him. Still, I feel like a total freak flipping off the walls of my apartment. God, I'm paranoid. And totally fucked. I'm totally, totally fucked.

Heath doesn't come the next night either, though not without texting to make sure I know where he is. It's weirdly sweet. He says Max, who I assume is his crime partner or whatever, isn't doing well, and that he really needs to stay with him. Plus, he says he has a lot of work. Whatever the hell that means.

The soreness in my pussy from all the fucking and fingering the last few days has finally subsided, and honestly, I really want to fucking touch myself. It's been a long two days at work, trying to flesh out Heath's weird robber idea for a marketing pitch. Dylan actually doesn't think it's horrible. He says we could take a comical spin on it, and that it might get people talking.

I'm working away on a presentation, piecing together a coherent proposal, confirming all the tiny details. It's coming together relatively smoothly, but Dylan keeps breathing down my neck. At first, I think he's just interested in the pitch, but then it hits me: it's probably about something else entirely.

It's been over a week and a half since our last inappropriate "meeting," and I'm positive he's noticed. We usually hook up at least once a week, sometimes twice, and I've definitely fallen behind on our little arrangement.

Not that I care too much about hooking up with him. It's always more about focusing on trying to come than actually enjoying it. But it's crucial to keep up those extra "credit points" if I want to maintain my standing. Earlier today, before lunch, I considered popping into his office—thought I might offer a little stress relief session—but I stopped myself.

In mere days, Heath has stormed into my life so explosively that it feels like a solidified rule now: he's the only one I'm relieving stress with. If Heath doesn't want me using dildos, he sure as hell wouldn't want me playing with another actual dick, and for some reason, I feel like I owe it to him to respect that.

Maybe it's because he's a dangerous criminal who carries a knife, or even a gun, and tracks my every move.

So, I don't go to Dylan's office. I decide against it, a bit confused and concerned for myself for choosing a literal criminal over the guy I've been casually seeing for months. Now, sitting on my couch with a glass of wine in hand, I ponder my life choices. The apartment feels oddly empty—I've kind of gotten used to Heath just being here.

Suddenly, the doorbell rings, startling me. My heart races. Maybe Heath's done with work or whatever the hell he's been doing with Max and decided to show up. But as I press the buzzer to open the main door, I remember—Heath never uses the doorbell.

Peeking through the peephole, I'm curious and slightly terrified about who might be coming up. I don't have many friends, and we rarely get guests in this part of town, so this person's identity is a complete mystery.

When I spot the familiar mop of black hair bobbing up the stairs, my heart beats even faster—and not in a good way.

I open the door to find Dylan standing in the hallway, holding a bottle of wine with a smile plastered on his face.

**14**

—  •  —

## CHAPTER 14

G ISELE

"Campbell," he greets me kindly. "You're home."

"I am," I confirm, feeling my irritation creep in.

"May I come in?"

I want to say no. I don't want him in my apartment. It's not that I don't trust him—I just don't want him here, and I definitely don't want to deal with rejecting his advances tonight.

"How did you know where I live?" I ask, suddenly realizing he's never been here before.

He shrugs, a slight blush on his cheeks. "I'm your boss, Gisele. I have your W-9."

The explanation sounds creepier than he probably intends, but I ignore it, stepping aside to let him in. Dylan isn't dangerous. I know that.

And considering I'm fucking a robber-slash-stalker, I'm not really in a position to judge how safe my choices are.

Besides, if I refuse him entry, he'll ask why, and then things will get awkward at work, and there goes any hope of a raise.

Maybe I can fake having my period or something. Have a glass of wine with him, and then send him on his way.

Dylan follows me into the kitchen area, setting the bottle of wine on the counter. As he steps forward, he accidentally kicks something on the floor, sending it skidding to a stop near my slipper. I glance down.

"What's that?" he asks, sounding genuinely puzzled.

I shrug. "No idea. Looks like a roach trap. Probably something the old tenants left behind."

Though I know that's not true. I've lived here for years, and it doesn't look like an old trap. Plus, I've noticed fewer of those little pests around lately. My little thief has washed my dishes before, so maybe this is his doing, too. The thought makes me smile. I kick the trap back under the fridge.

Dylan perches on the back of the couch, right where Heath fucked me last time. My body tingles at the memory, making me momentarily lose my train of thought.

"You've been a little distant lately," he says, tilting his head slightly. "I know you've been working hard. I thought we could relax a bit. Have a drink."

I force a small smile, trying to mask my discomfort. I uncork the bottle he brought, pouring some into the glass I've already been using, then fill another for him.

The entire time, my mind is buzzing with questions. How long do I entertain this? How long before I send him packing and avoid whatever conversation he's trying to initiate?

I hand him the glass, my smile more of a forced grimace now.

We're making small talk—menial, uninteresting drivel about work, then a bit about life. Dylan makes a few dull attempts to get to know me better, as if he doesn't already know just about everything from our years of working together. I feel my eyelids drooping; it's a struggle to keep my eyes open.

Is Dylan handsome? Yes, absolutely. One hundred percent.

Is he good at his job? Without a doubt. Two hundred percent.

But is he also the most basic, boring man on the planet, desperately masking his intent to get a blow job from his subordinate under the guise of wine and casual chitchat? Oh, yeah. Three hundred percent.

I'm forcing smile after smile, nodding my head every few seconds like a puppet, pretending to listen as he rambles on about some mundane office drama. My face hurts from all the fake grinning, and my patience is running dangerously thin.

I can't even bring myself to care what he's talking about; the sound of his voice is just a dull buzz in my ears.

I start thinking about how long I have to keep this charade up before I can kick him out without it becoming a whole thing at work tomorrow.

And then, the door bursts open.

My head snaps toward the entrance, and a wave of relief washes over me. It's like a light switch flipping in my brain—I've never been so fucking grateful to have my apartment broken into.

Heath stands in the doorway, head-to-toe in black, from his boots to the ski mask with a skull imprint. I can't help but smile.

Dylan jumps out of his seat with a yelp, staring at me, caught off guard. He must've seen the smile on my face, and I quickly switch to a look of utter fear and shock, trying to play along with whatever the hell Heath has in mind.

Heath strides over to Dylan without a word, grabs him by the shirt, and hurls him across the room like he's weightless. Dylan slams against the far wall, crumpling to the floor with a groan.

Then, without missing a beat, Heath yanks me by the back of the head, pulling me close to stare into my eyes. I widen my gaze at him, putting on my best sweet and innocent look, silently apologizing for being such a "bad, bad girl."

A low growl rumbles from his chest as he drags me out from behind the counter. We end up standing behind the couch, facing Dylan, who is now cowering on the floor. Heath slaps my ass hard, shoving me over the cushions.

"Hey!" Dylan shouts, his voice shaky.

Heath shoots him a glare that could cut glass, and Dylan shrinks back, practically merging with the floor. Heath turns his attention away from me, pulling a gun from his pocket, flicking the blade open with a metallic snap as he advances on my boss.

I scream. He literally brought a gun this time! Not knife. A fucking gun!

"Shh" Heath signs me and shifts his attention back to Dylan. "If I said I was going to fuck her right here," Heath says, crouching down in front of a trembling Dylan, "what would you do?"

"Please, don't hurt me!" Dylan squeaks, his eyes glued to the gun.

"Pathetic." Heath scoffs, gripping Dylan's shirt and hauling him up off the floor. His other hand wraps tightly around Dylan's throat. "Wrong answer, Jones."

"W-what are you going to do to me?" Dylan stammers, his voice barely audible.

"To you?" Heath chuckles darkly, tilting his head back in a laugh that feels like it reverberates through the walls. "Nothing. Not right now, at least. But you'll pay for what you've been doing to her. I know all your dirty little secrets."

Dylan's eyes dart to me, wide and pleading. At this point, I'm perched on the back of the couch, enjoying the unfolding scene with mild interest. Heath's mention of "secrets" catches my attention.

"Secrets?" I ask, my curiosity piqued.

Heath again shoots me a look over his shoulder, his jaw clenched. "I'll deal with you next," he snaps. His anger is palpable, simmering beneath the surface. But it kind of turns me on.

"What are you going to do to her?" Dylan asks again, his voice breaking.

Heath's lips curl into a dangerous smile. "I'm going to fuck her. Are you planning to stop me?"

Dylan's mouth falls open, but no words come out. He's frozen, terrified, unable to respond. Heath pockets the knife, tears the mask off his face, and Dylan's eyes go wide with shock, recognizing him.

"You don't have to stop me," Heath says, voice low and menacing. "She wants it." With that, he hauls Dylan up by the collar again, dragging him to the door. He shoves my boss out into the hallway like he's tossing out the trash. "Better get going, Dylan. We're usually pretty loud." He slams the door shut in Dylan's face.

"You'll regret this!" Dylan shouts from the other side of the door, sounding more pitiful than threatening.

I stand there, catching my breath, watching as Heath slowly turns to face me. His eyes are wild, burning with a mix of fury and something darker.

I rush toward him, ready to jump into his arms, but he pushes me right down on the couch. I bounce a little on the couch as I fall back.

"Heath!" I attempt to pick my upper body up, but he stands right in front of me, places a foot on the couch right beside me, and pushes me back again.

His elbow rests on his knee. His hands lock my wrists above my head. He's got me completely trapped, and the look on his face sends a thrill through my entire body.

"You," he growls, eyes narrowing. "You will entertain no one else. Understood?"

"What did you mean about secrets?" I manage to ask, my voice barely a whisper.

His grip tightens on my wrists. "I'll tell you when you deserve to know. You don't get to give away what's mine." He rips off his gloves, throwing them aside. One hand wraps around my throat, the other pries my mouth open. "This," he says, putting two fingers in my mouth, "is mine."

I swallow hard, nodding frantically as his fingers dig into my jaw. "I promise," I choke out, garbling the words. "Nothing happened."

His face hovers just above mine, his nose brushing against mine.

"And it never will," he says, his voice a dangerous whisper, "He wouldn't have left alive if something happened"

## 15

### CHAPTER 15

G ISELE

He crushes his lips to mine, biting down hard as he kisses me. I moan into his mouth, my hands clawing at his clothes, desperate to feel his skin.

He drags me to my feet, bending me over the counter. His palm comes down on my ass with a loud slap, and I scream as the cold surface bites into my hips. The countertop is too high; my feet dangle off the ground as he presses his weight against me.

"You're moving in with me tonight," he growls, thrusting into me from behind. "It's safer there. He won't be able to just drop by."

"I'm not moving in with you!" I shout, gasping for breath as he fucks me hard.

He laughs, a deep, dark sound. "You don't want to be kept by a man who fucks you like this?"

"I don't want to be kidnapped by a fucking stalker!" I shriek, writhing under his grip. "You're insane if you think I will."

He chuckles darkly, his hand winding into my hair and yanking my head back. "Maybe I am insane," he whispers into my ear. "But you're mine, and I'm never letting you go."

I whimper, biting down on my lip as his pace quickens, his thrusts becoming erratic. "Are you going to come, Gisele?" he taunts, his voice dripping with dark amusement. "You want to come for me?"

"Yes," I gasp. "Please, Heath, please—"

"That's too fucking bad," he growls, pulling out abruptly. The emptiness is unbearable, and I scream in frustration.

He grabs my chin, forcing me to look at him. "Beg me," he orders, his eyes boring into mine. "Beg me, and I might let you come."

"Please," I whisper, my voice cracking. "Please, Heath, I need it. I need you."

"I was watching you," he bites out, his voice a rough snarl. "You were smiling at him."

"That was all an act. And... Y-you have cameras?!" I try to ask.

"One in your bedroom, one in the living room," he says, his hips slamming against me. "I was checking up on you, ready to come tell you what I found about your raise. And then I saw him here." His hand comes down on my ass again, harder this time.

"You're mine," he whispers against my lips. "My beautiful, sweet Gisele. I am forever lost in you."

I nod, wrapping my arms around his neck, still aching for release. I try to push him down, wanting to ride his face, but he resists, pulling back with a teasing smile. "So impatient," he murmurs, lifting me to my feet. "Pack your most important things. I'll come back for the rest."

And just like that, he's gone, slipping into the bathroom, leaving me on the floor, shaking, wanting more, and entirely at his mercy.

HEATH

I stand Gisele's suitcase next to me at the front door of the apartment and cover her eyes with both hands. She's already made a few approving comments about the neighborhood, and I can't wait to see how happy she'll be when she sees the inside of our home.

My dad did a nice job picking this place. It is one of the properties he owns. I never let anyone come over, but the thought of sharing it with Gisele makes my heart flip like a pancake.

I'm still annoyed about the whole Dylan thing, but I can hardly help the urge to jump up and down with excitement over bringing my Gisele home.

As I reach for my keys, I realize I've left one of her eyes uncovered. "Fuck." I want it to be a surprise.

I grab my mask from my pocket, shove it onto her head, ignoring her slight protest, and twist it around so the eyeholes sit at the back.

Then, I unlock the door, lead her inside, and place her suitcase by the kitchen counter before closing the door behind us. Grabbing the top of the mask, I pull it up, unveiling her face from beneath a fluffy mess of dark, ruffled hair.

She glowers at me for only a moment before her eyes widen, and she starts raking her gaze over the apartment. "Holy shit, Heath."

She takes a few steps across the black flooring, running a hand over the sparkling kitchen counter and peering into the living room area to the right, entirely encased in floor-to-ceiling windows. I imagine us sitting together on the black couch, watching movies, snacks piled high on the sleek, white coffee table.

Looking to her left, she approaches the bedroom area. It's all open concept but perfectly separated and private enough.

As she touches the sheets on the bed, I picture rolling around with her on it for the first time. I can't fucking wait for it, though I remind myself she's still learning her lesson and isn't allowed to come yet.

Still, I'm excited. A guy can punish his girlfriend and be excited at the same time, right?

"Heath, I just don't know," she says, walking back towards the kitchen area, illuminated by the warm overhead lights and the city view through the windows behind her.

"What don't you know?" I take her face in my hands and cock my head.

"We've hardly known each other a week. It seems too soon to move in together."

"You had sex with a robber who stalks you, and now you're questioning whether it's too soon to move in together?"

She shakes her head, rearing it back in shock. "Heath, that's the most lucid thing you've ever said to me."

I chuckle and reach one hand down the front of her pants, circling her clit. She tenses immediately, clinging to me with a whimper.

"I know I'm an unconventional man," I say casually. "I know our relationship started in an unconventional way."

"Relationship?" she breathes, little squeaks escaping her lips as I sink two fingers into her and press my palm against her clit.

"But that doesn't mean you don't like me. And I do like you." A lot more than like, actually.

"Fuck, Heath," she moans, grinding her hips into my hand.

"Different isn't bad, my sweet gift. Didn't you hear? We live on a floating rock. Nothing matters. Nothing except you."

Her pussy clamps around my fingers, and my cock strains against the zipper of my pants. Fuck, I want to watch her come so fucking badly, but I'm still upset she let that fucking loser manipulator into her old house.

Just when I'm sure she's about to break, I remove my hand and lick my fingers clean. So fucking delicious. "Heath!" she cries, falling into me and rubbing her thighs together.

I put my hands on her hips and tilt my head to one side in reprimand. "You weren't even listening to me, were you?"

She pretends to sob into my chest, whining and groaning. I giggle and kiss her on the head before hopping off to grab her suitcase.

We walk to the bedroom area, and I pull her into the walk-in closet, presenting my work to her. I've moved all my things to the left side of every shelf and rack, leaving her exactly half.

She wanders in as if she's standing in front of one of the natural wonders of the world, her eyes sparkling as she looks all around, drinking in the sight.

"When did you do this?" she whispers.

I shrug. "A few nights ago."

"A few nights ag—" Her eyebrows crinkle at me. "Heath, we met on Monday. It's only Friday."

"True love waits for no one."

"That's not the saying, Heath, that—ugh." She slaps a hand to her forehead. "Were you ever going to give me a choice? I know you're... unconventional. But, when it really came down to it, if I had looked you in the eye and told you I didn't want you, would you have let me say no?"

My head rears back at the question. She's never spoken to me this way before. She sounds so genuine. "Of course, I'd let you say no. I do the things you like, Gisele. I thought you liked me this way."

"I do, but I... I did say no, Heath. I told you very clearly that I didn't want you."

I try to smile, but her words hurt. It feels like someone is pressing a needle into my poor heart. "I watch you very carefully to make sure that I... I only want to make you feel good. I didn't believe you when you said that. Were you being truthful?"

"I—" She pauses. "I guess at the time... I don't know."

I take a step toward her, running two fingers down her hair with care, sharp tears threatening my eyes. "Do you want to leave?"

It would break my heart, but she's speaking in earnest. I could steal as much of her as I wanted, but what good is it if she doesn't love me as I do her?

She takes far too long to answer, and my chest starts caving in.

"No," she finally says. "I guess I don't."

She doesn't love me.

A tear roll down my cheek.

She raises her eyebrows, "I guess I don't want to leave? Sir?"

Oh.

My grin eats up my face again, and I scoop her into my arms, carrying her to the bed and tossing her onto it. My girl has just earned herself the right to come, and I eat that delicious pussy until she does it twice.

**16**

## CHAPTER 16

G ISELE

I watch Heath chopping vegetables and tossing them into a boiling pot as I make my way around every square foot of his—our?—place, observing the dark details and sleek lines.

It looks like a goddamn hotel, not some freaky dungeon. The dude is apparently fucking loaded. He probably has all kinds of weird secret bank accounts and shit.

But what really gets me is the collection of photos scattered around his home. For the first time, it hits me that Heath is a whole person. A whole person with a family, maybe friends, and twenty-four years of life that I know absolutely nothing about.

I become entirely fixated on the string of frames atop a dark oak side table.

"Is that a husky?" I ask, pointing at one of the photos showing a beautiful black and white dog in front of a line of trees. I turn towards the kitchen to face him.

He smiles. "Yes."

"Is it yours?"

"Mhm." He nods proudly. "That's Max."

"Max," I repeat with a smile, then my face straightens out in an instant. "Wait a second. You said you were working late. You were with Max. Is your boss' name Max too?"

"Baby." He shakes his head. "I am the boss. It's the same Max. I was with him." He nudges his forehead towards the photo.

My eyebrows furrow. "Max is a dog?"

"Does that surprise you? I've told you twice now that I work with animals. The only boss here other than me is my dad."

Wait a second. What the fuck? No. He can't mean real animals. He must be talking about outlaws, heathens, or something like that.

"You're a thief," I say, as if trying to convince him of his own profession.

"I'm not a thief. I run my father's business. An organisation which is... eh, not so legal but yeah. It is much more bigger than robbing houses."

My mouth drops open. He never mentioned these things. All this time I was thinking he is a thief. "Then... why did you try robbing my house?"

"I wasn't actually robbing, baby. We got news that there were some important documents we needed, but that was a mistake. The best mistake happened to me."

I walk over to the kitchen area, where he remains at the stove, wooden spoon in hand, looking at me with a lazy smile, as if I'm the crazy one.

"Okay, but... why do you keep a gun?"

He told me his business isn't so legal one. But does he really keep a gun with him usually? Is it that dangerous? I press my lips together.

"Well," he corrects, tilting his head to the side. "Technically, it is to keep myself safe."

I blink hard, confusion thickening in my throat. "Safe from what?"

"From danger."

"Uh? You kill people?"

"I haven't killed many people."

I gasp, "Means you have killed few?"

He places the wooden spoon over the pot he's stirring and chuckles. "Gisele." He seriously thinks I'm the crazy one.

"What?! I'm not a stalker like you. I don't just know every-thing about you."

"Uhm, no, but listen to me. I couldn't ignore it when they had a gun pointed at my sister. My father used to have some super big name in underground world. Not criminals or shits like that. Much, much bigger than that. He used to have big connections. And big connections bring big dangers. He also runs multiple businesses, and after marrying my mother, he basically focused on business only. For safety of us. I'm just helping him in this. It's all mine after him. It's ours."

"What businesses are you talking about?"

"Real estate, a dozen of gyms, a dozen of bars around whole country."

"That's insane money." I blurt.

"It is. After those incidents got my mother kidnapped by insane people, we basically stayed away from illegal stuff. We still have to stay safe and protect ourselves. Now we are a happy family, will take you to meet them soon."

"Oh no... was your mom safe?" I can't help but ask. Genuinely concerned. And he wants me to meet his family already? Such men exist?

"She was fine. She is a martial arts expert. Handled them all."

Sounds like very powerful family...

"Okay, I'm sorry. Thanks for explaining things." I smile but feel my hand shivering a bit, seeing the gun kept at the table nearby couch.

It's scary. Knife? I was okay with that, but a gun is very big thing. I heard the gunshot sounds when I was a kid, and it left me childhood trauma. The gun was pointed at no one but my own father.

"Gisele? What's bothering you?"

"The gun..." I tell honestly.

"Are you afraid?" he asks, "I won't ever hurt you, baby"

"I know... but..."

"Do you want me to keep it aside in my locker?" I look at him, he seriously would do that for him? He takes my silence as yes, and picks the gun before disappearing in one of the rooms, before coming back to me.

"Now good?" he questions smiling, so unbothered by the thing my fear made him do.

"Thanks..."

"Anything for you, my gift."

"And the gift thing?" I ask again, my forearms slumped on the cold counter, "Why do you always call me that?"

He blushes. This man actually fucking blushes. "Because you are a gift."

"Heath, you don't even know me."

"I know, I know." He looks genuinely lucid for once. "My mom used to say that if we do good things, life would give us little gifts. Karma, I guess. And on the hard days, we just had to remember those gifts were coming. I'd been having a really tough few months because of my father, Gisele. He's a really tough man when it comes to me, he expects me to be strong and tough but I end up doing stupidity. I try but it will take time. And then you showed up. I saw you and thought, This is it. Finally. It's her."

For a moment, I just stare at him in silence—at this beautiful, absurd man cooking me dinner, rambling about how much he is expected to do from his family is sad. His heart isn't stoney, he can't act tough always. He is such a sweet person. Sweet hearted. Not made for such things. He doesn't deserve to have to constantly protect himself and his family.

"Are you like... certifiably fucking insane?" I finally blurt out. No judgment, just real, pure curiosity.

His smile grows impossibly wide, stretching from cheek to cheek. "I don't know. I've never been assessed."

**17**

**CHAPTER 17**

H EATH

Gisele giggles for me all night. If watching her come is incredible, then watching her laugh is straight-up fucking mesmerizing.

It's Friday night, nearing 11:00 p.m. She doesn't have work tomorrow, I can do whatever I want, and we're free to just...hang out. Sure, I kind of miss sneaking in and scaring the shit out of her, but there will be plenty of opportunities for that.

For now, I'm happy with her scooped up in my arms as we waddle around the kitchen, looking for treats to bring over to the couch to watch TV and snack together.

I pick her up by her hips so she can kneel on the counter and reach a high cabinet, resisting the urge to drop down and eat her up as she sits there. She's at such a perfect height for it.

Instead, I twist her long, dark hair in my fingers, pulling it into different hairstyles as she rummages.

"So many beans," she says, plucking through cans.

"You don't get a body this nice from just drinking wine and eating pasta," I say.

"I do," she retorts, looking over her shoulder to smirk at me. I bite her delt playfully, eyes locked on hers.

"Do you work out?" she asks, turning back towards the cabinet.

I clutch a hand to my heart in mock offense. "You've wounded me."

She giggles again, and I drink up those fucking sounds.

"I do," I answer. "Mixed martial arts, mostly. I did bōjutsu in college too. But my mom started teaching me martial arts when I was very young, it used to my favourite."

"Sweet. You went to college?" she asks, as if I've just told her I've been to the moon.

"I did. For computer science. Is it so hard to believe that criminals are educated?"

"No. It's just that you're so fucking stupid, I assumed—"

Before she can finish that sentence, I drag her off the counter.

"You're gonna pay for that."

She yelps and giggles, kicking at me as best she can. My joy can hardly be contained. She's laughing, teasing, making jokes. She's... comfortable.

Gisele wrestles her way down onto the floor, and I bend over her before she can get away, wrapping my hand around her ankle and lifting her by one leg as if she's a sack of trash.

At first, she continues to wriggle and squeal, but soon realizes it's pointless and lets her body fall slack.

My silly girl is begging to be punished.

I haul her into the bathroom and tear her clothes off of her until she stands stark naked before me, her feet pressing into the dark gray tiles. She's still smiling. I cock my head at that, enjoying it while it lasts, which won't be for long.

Ripping open the glass door of the large shower, I shove her in and press her back against the freezing wall, stepping in with her so she can't escape.

"Fuck, Heath!" she screeches in protest, her grin falling from her face as she arches off the cold surface. She immediately begins shivering, her skin pricking with goosebumps.

I lean down to her ear, taking a moment to nuzzle my nose into her hair and inhale the scent of her shampoo. "It's about to get a lot worse," I promise.

Keeping one hand around her neck, I reach for the shower hose, pull it off the hook, and flick on the water, turning the nozzle to the cold setting.

"No, no, no, Heath!"

I turn the water on her face, soaking her head and hair. It drips over my wrist and the stretch of my sweatshirt on my forearm. Fuck, it's cold. Poor girl. She slips away and bolts to the far end of the shower, but I catch her, wrestling her into my body and drenching her more. I have to keep a tight grip on her. It's like holding onto a slippery fish.

"And you?" I ask over her squeals. Her body reels into mine, my sopping clothes probably only making her colder. "When are you going to tell me more about you?"

"Heath!" she gasps instead of answering. She's absolutely trembling.

Stubborn girl. I pull her up as straight as I can, covering her tits and stomach with frigid water as I watch it trickle down to her legs. Fuck, she looks so fucking delicious as she twists and kicks.

"I want you to tell me."

"Fuck! Fuck, fuck, ffffuck. There's not much t-to tell."

My face hardens. That kind of talk pisses me off. I turn the water away from her and press her back into the tiles again.

"Why the fuck do you have such a hard time understanding that I want to know about you?" I press my nose against hers. She feels like ice.

For a few moments, the only sound in the silence is the rush of water and her heavy breathing. She wheezes as she stares into my eyes.

"Answer me," I urge.

"I didn't... I didn't realize that I..."

She shakes her head, and my face softens as I come to. The girl has nothing to say. She has no idea who she is.

"Gisele, what do you like? Do you like cheerleading?" I've seen enough photos in the university archives to know that, at one point, she was the captain.

"No," she whispers.

"Then what do you like? One thing. It can be the littlest thing. I want to know."

GISELE

I blink, hot tears forming in my freezing eyes. Heath's questions are oddly intimate, and I don't expect the wave of emotion that washes over me. There's nothing I can even tell him.

I, as a human, have no details. No mixed martial arts, no vegetarianism. Nothing. It truly hadn't crossed my mind until now. Maybe I can tell him about my family.

But all I ever do is drink wine and masturbate. That isn't a lie. I go on runs, I go to work, and I go to bed. That's it. A happy little routine to get me from one end of the day to the other. I've been like that for as long as I can remember.

Sure, I go to meet my family and on the occasional date. I don't hate the attention. I do, however, hate that everything I do or say is nearly always misinterpreted. I hate that most people's biggest issues are shit like wasted potential and pants that don't quite fit right.

So, I keep things simple when it comes to chatting with others. Talk more about appropriate things like ponytails and hair clips.

"Tell me, Gisele," Heath urges once more.

I blurt out the first thing that comes to mind. "Clean sheets." I'll never forget when I finally learned how to use the washer and dryer and could clean my sheets whenever I wanted. It was like a little gift to myself.

Heath's eyebrows float up his forehead. I read that as pity, and I'm sure he's going to think it's silly, but instead, he says, "Then I will wash our sheets daily. Tell me another."

I swallow hard. God, thinking of one thing was difficult enough, but another?

"Uhm. My job." I do like it, and I'm good at it, despite being overworked and constantly subjected to some of the most vapid people on the planet.

Heath's hand moves to touch the side of my head as he rubs his nose against mine. "Good. Not many people can say that. Another."

I think for a beat before answering, my attention fixed on his lips. "Music. Deathcore. It turns me on."

"Good." His body inches closer. "Another."

My breathing picks back up, my lungs inflating as if to near my hard nipples to Heath. "Cucumbers with salt and garlic powder."

"Another." His mouth hovers over mine.

"Rain on windows."

"Another."

"Cartoons."

"Another."

"You, Heath." I grab his head and crush my mouth to his, and he absolutely devours me. He groans as I grab his hair in both hands, sliding my fingers up his scalp.

He holds the water off to the side still, and his free hand trails down the length of my cold body, my senses on high alert. I wrap a leg around him, wishing he weren't so fully clothed. I want to feel his heat.

His tongue slides on mine, his lips wiping off any sting left behind by his teeth as he bites into me. Heath is pleasure and pain and, I'm starting to believe, the embodiment of my twisted, fucked-up homecoming to myself.

He pulls me in and spins me around, pressing my back into his front. His heavy clothing is a frozen blanket on my skin. Reaching his hands around me, he changes the setting on the shower head so it shoots in one thick stream. He does not change the temperature.

"Heath," I breathe as I watch. I can't handle any more cold. "Do you trust me?"

I shiver in his arms, staring at the water.

"Do you trust me?"

"Yes."

He kicks my legs apart and braces me with an arm around my ribs before turning the water on my clit. It beats against me, causing me to scream and squirm from the pressure. The cold seeps into me continuously, my skin somehow icing over even more, though I didn't think it possible.

"You can take it," he whispers. "Be a good girl."

"Heath!" My legs do their best to pull inward, to shield me, but it's no use. He has me hooked and parted with his ankles.

After a few long, trembling moments, the sensations between my legs subside slightly, and I'm numb. When my whimpers begin to weaken, Heath quickly turns off the water and drops the hose, spinning me around. He falls to his knees and grabs my thigh in one hand, lifting it over his shoulder. Then, his hot tongue falls to my freezing clit. The contrast has me keeling over, gripping his hair as I scream for him. It's warm and luscious and delicious in all the ways I crave.

I'm too fucking cold to relax into it fully, and I have a feeling that's part of this little game.

Pushing his head away from me, I turn for only a split second before he snatches me again. But I've already grabbed the hose. I wrestle against his attempts, turning the water on as we slip and slide on the shower floor.

"Bad girl," he chides, his smile wide. I turn the hose at him, and he scrambles back on the tiles, laughing like a madman.

"Fuck. You," I bite out through chattering teeth.

He rips his drenched clothes off under the stream of freezing liquid until he lays there naked and grinning. "You won't be able to if my dick is numb."

I cock my head, turning the water to a softer rain setting, holding it right over his groin. "Let's see how fucking small you get."

"Ha!" Heath shoots up and wraps his arms around my legs, pulling me down on the floor with him. The water sprays up the glass toward the ceiling as I fall. He holds me down in a hug and kicks a foot up to make the water warmer as the cold tiles dig into my bones.

I go to turn the warm water on myself, but he quickly blurts, "Don't!" For a moment, I lie there shivering in his arms. "Check it with my hand first. You could burn yourself."

I do as he says, but why his hand? Isn't he way too sweet? I wait until the water feels comfortable before showering both of us in it. Fuck, it feels divine as it melts away every bit of cold discomfort.

He kicks his foot up again and pulls on a lever under the temperature control with his toes. Hot water begins to fall straight from the ceiling. I release the hose and ease into the warm comfort, kissing him under the rain.

Heath grabs every inch of me, biting and licking at my wet skin, running his fingers down my side and trailing them between my legs. It's uncharacteristically sensual.

We remain completely entangled on the floor, inching closer and closer to each other, body and soul, taking our sweet time to warm up and turn on.It feels like a fucking dream as we lay there covered in steam. My heart thrums in my chest for this man, my body feeling all kinds of sensations I've never experienced before.

**18**

## CHAPTER 18

GISELE

After our shower, Heath dries my hair with a blow dryer he says hasn't been used in a year. Not since his own hair reached his shoulders. I decide I wouldn't have minded seeing him like that.

He then gives me his largest sweatshirt and accompanying sweatpants, wrapping me in his clean sheets like a cozy burrito before slipping in next to me.

"I didn't know you wear glasses," I say, noting the thin, wire frames he has placed on his nose while I was changing.

He smiles. "My optometrist would kill me if she knew how often I wear my contacts in the shower." I don't know why, but the glasses kind of do it for me. "Want to see something funny?" he asks with a snort, leaning up against the headboard with his phone in front of his face.

His black T-shirt clings to him, tattoos crawling down his forearms like vines.

"Yeah."

"I got a notification that someone entered your old house." My eyes widen, partially at the shocking change of subject and partially at the fact he is already calling it my old house. He shrugs casually. "Motion sensors. Check it out."

I lean up and look at his screen to find a view of my living room from atop the fridge. Two police officers stand by the couch with Dylan, who flails his arms silently. It seems he is trying to explain what went down.

"Can you turn on the sound?" I ask.

Heath shakes his head. "Only video."

"No sound? God, you're like the worst stalker ever."

"Well, sorry for trying to give you a bit of privacy." He scoffs, nudging himself further into the pillow behind his back. I smile and lay my cheek on his shoulder.

"Gisele, I have to, uhm... I have to tell you something about Dylan."

My head immediately shoots back up. "Oh yeah! What was all that? You said he had secrets? He is totally harmless."

In the last few days of knowing Heath, I've never seen him nervous. Not even for a second. But now, he truly seems worried. Like he doesn't quite know how to express his thoughts to me.

"I hacked your firm's system and put in a request for you to get a raise, acting as Dylan."

"Heath Steinfeld!" I smack him on the shoulder in reprimand, and his grin grows wide with a chuckle.

"Did you just scold me, little Gisele?"

I shrug and click my tongue. "Maybe. Now spit it out."

"Right, uhm. I emailed Mr. Eve, your CEO."

"Mr. Evans."

"Right, Mr. Evans. And he replied saying that they couldn't accommodate the request, given your recent raise in January."

My heart trips over itself. "My what? I didn't get a raise."

"I know. I sifted through every record. Your pay has been the same since you started that role. It wasn't until I looked into the bills for other employees' salaries that I found the discrepancy. All their payments are approved by Shelley Meyers from finance."

"Sweet girl."

"Yours are approved by Dylan Jones. They always have been."

My head cocks. I am hardly catching on. "So, what are you implying?"

"Gisele, you got a raise. He's been paying you a fraction of your salary and taking the difference."

A heavy weight pulls my shoulders down to the floor, my neck extending in utter defense. "What? No. That's not possible."

"I even saw your original contract. He changed the salary on it, and that's what he presented to you. He's been doing it since you were promoted."

"No," I say with a chuckle. "No, absolutely not." I shake my head back and forth, my throat closing up quickly.

But Heath fetches his laptop, pulls up the records and, lo and behold, it is all right there. Right down to Dylan's original request to Shelley that he'd be approving my bills, given the seniority of my position. She was a fucking idiot to believe that, but it doesn't surprise me.

Rage boils in my gut, my face and ears overheating. The asshole has been smiling innocently at me for two years. We are fucking team members. We had a fucking professional relationship. Not to mention, he has quite literally been fucking me. All this time I thought I had the upper hand, and that is just fucking embarrassing.

"I could kill him!" I shriek.

"We will," Heath says with an empathetic smile, placing his hand on my cheek. "Not really, unless you want to." He shrugs. "But we will teach him a lesson, my sweet gift. A very important one."

I shake my head in disbelief. At this point, that doesn't sound like the worst idea. For the first time this week, I am truly grateful that Heath is terrifying. Not just because it turns me on, but because we are gonna get this guy. Oh, we are so gonna fucking get this guy.

"Don't worry, baby. I promise we'll fix it. You won't just get that raise, you'll get his fucking job."

I blow out a puff of air and cross my arms. "I can't believe he would do that to me."

A creepy smile melts across Heath's cheeks. "Think about it this way. He's at your house panicking, and you're here, getting fucked like the goddess you are." A low, maniacal laugh bubbles up his throat, growing with each passing second as he presses his nose to mine. "Do you know what I'd like very much, baby?"

"What?" I breathe, inching backward. He looms over me on all fours, becoming increasingly wild.

"For him to have to watch the surveillance footage of us. I want him to see you on your knees, sobbing as you choke on my cock. We'll take everything from him. I promise you that."

My pussy clenches at the thought, Heath's body on top of mine. He tosses his phone to the side, seizes my face with his large hand, and drags one long lick from the base of my neck up to my cheek.

I roll my lip under my teeth, my mouth quirking up into a smile. Perhaps Heath's madness is contagious.

I kiss him and then immediately escape to run away. I want to piss him off again. He is rather good at punishments, and I am in the mood for a painful distraction.

Besides, I need to take back some power. I'd be lying if I said the news about Dylan don't make me feel utterly used.

Heath chuckles evilly and hops onto the floor behind me, but I am already halfway to the closet. I enter the walk-in and turn quickly to shut the door, clicking the lock shut and effectively trapping Heath on the other side, destroying his amusement.

"Gisele!" He pounds on the door. "What the hell are you doing, my beautiful gift?" His voice is so desperate. I like that.

"Any chance you have cameras in your own house?" I ask playfully. "Of course, I do. Why do you ask?"

"Your thought about Dylan gave me an idea." I smile and run a hand down the door, teasing the poor guy through the wood.

"No," he breathes as he backs away. The bed sounds with a quick bounce and I assume he is grabbing his phone. I turn my back to the door and let my body slide down to the floor. Once again, the sound of Heath's movement nears me, and he groans. He has likely just opened up the surveillance to find me running my fingers over my body. "No. Please, baby, please."

Too late.

I reach both hands to the hem of my sweatshirt and pull it off, feeling the air on my tits. "Baby, please," he begs once more.Hooking my thumbs into the hem of the sweatpants, I push them over my legs and pop them off my ankles, sitting on the floor completely naked. It isn't clear where the cameras are, though I suppose that's the point of secret surveillance. I reach a hand between my legs and begin circling my wet clit. With my free hand, I grab my tit, squeezing it hard."Oh my god!" I moan, leaning my head back into the surface behind me.

"Luna!"I smile. He sounds very angry."Oh, fuck yes! Oh god!" I squeal. I am exaggerating, of course. But truth be told, his desperation is so fucking hot, and it really does feel good. "Very bad girl," he bites. "You'll regret this."I don't know what he is up to, but I am sure it would be good. For the time being, I simply enjoy myself. My fingers sink past my clit and into my sopping pussy, hooking up to hit that incredible spot. It had been so long since I've touched myself and, while I didn't need any more orgasms, I can't say I didn't enjoy it.

Heath's voice sound behind me once again. "Back away from the fucking door."My lip roll beneath my teeth. Good boy. I pull my fingers from between my legs and shift over to a better spot before returning my attention to my clit, touching myself as Heath picks the lock and burst into the walk-in.Fuck, the rage in his features is so fucking hot.

The man is absolutely boiling, his eyes wide as he stalks toward me.In an instant, he grabs me by my arms and hauls me to my feet, shoving me over to a closet rack. He reaches into a shelf and pulls out a belt, forcing my wrists above my head to tie me to the rod on which his clothing hangs, push into an opening between some jackets. I stand there, stark naked, leather biting into my wrists.

He laughs at the sight.I kick a foot out frustratedly, my heel making contact with his ribs. His face drops, icy flames in his eyes as he grabs my ankle and pulls on me until I lost my footing. He bundles me up in his arms, wrapping my legs around his waist. "You wanna fucking play, little girl?"Suddenly, Heath rams me into the wall behind me, the leather pulling at my wrists, and I squeal."Fight back," he orders, knowing I can't possibly.

I kick my legs and he quickly moves his arms to hold them in place, easily resisting my attempts. "Kick and scream all you want, baby. I am going to fuck you so fucking hard, and there's not a thing you can do about it."

**19**

— • —

## CHAPTER 19

G ISELE

I can't help the smirk that takes my face. I probably look something like Heath when he gets feral and amused. Like The Joker or some kind of freaky clown.

"You like that?" he asks. "You like that there's nothing you can fucking do about it?"

I whimper, nodding my head.

He chuckles, releasing me to let me stand on the ground before backing away. "That was a very, very bad thing to do, Gisele. Locking me out like that." He pulls his black T-shirt off completely, and then his gray sweatpants down so they sit around his strong thighs. "I should do the same to you."

He begins stroking his cock, groaning as he rakes his eyes over me, using me for his pleasure. "Fuck." Throaty, little moans escape him. He steps up to me and slaps one of my tits before pinching my nipple hard, and I screech. "I should leave you hanging here all night so I can come in every hour and fuck you. Would you like that, baby?"

My legs clench together on instinct, my body begging for him to end this fucking torture. I can't pry my gaze away from that perfect fucking cock, or the way his strong hands look as he strokes it, or how his arms flex beneath those fucking tattoos.

"Heath," I whin.

"Greedy girl," he bites, pressing himself into me once again. "You're lucky I want to fuck you so badly."

Heath slams his cock into me roughly, holding me against the wall. He leans into my ear as his tip touch my G-spot. "Try to stop me," he teases. "Try your hardest."

My body writhes under his hold. "You're much less scary with those glasses on," I say in an attempt to poke fun, but he proves me wrong, chuckling in my face and fucking me even harder.

"Be a good fucking girl and come for me." He removes his hands from my legs and props me on his hips, grabbing my face and jerking my head toward him. "Look me in the eye." My mouth parts, a moan escaping from deep in my chest as I stare into those icy blues. I can't help it. My body reacts to this man as if he built me himself. As if he knows every button and lever and exactly what it does and how it would make me react. I crumble for him entirely, clamping around his cock as my arms stiffens in their binds. Heath moans as he finds his release, the string connecting our gazes feeling very real and very tangible. HEATH

Gisele balls up in our bed, enveloped in my clothes and sheets. I lay next to her, watching as she sinks her head into the pillow, exhausted from the long day. Her eyes falls shut, and I dim the lights.

I'd rest soon too. For now, I just want to lay with her.

I run a finger through her hair, incapable of comprehending how a person can be so beautiful, how I've possibly gotten so lucky as to meet my wild match.

"I was so done with guys my age" she says quietly through the short, darksilence.

"Hm?" I crinkle an eyebrow, my touch trailing lazily to her sh oulder."I got cheated by my boyfriend. Manipulated. Abused. I thought he loved me. It all continued like that until my brother got to know about it."

My face slackens when I realized what she is doing. My beautifulgift. Oh, my beautiful, beautiful gift is sharing with me. Opening up tome. I listen silently.

"I never thought Archie could do something like that. He was never aggressive, always avoided fighting. But when he found out about him, he went to his home and beat him to pulp. Then I realised, I was surrounded with such gentle yet masculine men in household; how could I let that fragile, egoistic man manipulate me into thinking I don't deserve good treatment? I was so dumb."

My fist clenches. She doesn't deserve anything less than Queen treatment. Good her brother protected her in my absence.

"That day I decided, I won't ever love a man unless he treats like my father and brother  does. I never planned to let anyone in..."

I hope I treat her even better than them. I have no idea how did they treat her?

Her family isn't richy-rich type of family, loaded with shit tons of money, so I guess it isn't about loading her with luxury gifts. It is about treating her respectfully. My shoulders widened, I treat her very respectfully, everywhere, except the bed.

I swallow hard, ready to ask a question, hoping I wouldn't hate her answer. "Why did you let me in, though?" I'm also her age.

I want her to say because I am different, or because we are a match,or because I'm so fucking handsome, or because she simply can't help herself because the first time she saw me, she just knew.

She doesn't say any of those things. Instead, she wraps an arm around my waist, "You forced your way in."

My heart sinks. That isn't good enough for me. I need her to elaborate, and if the answer breaks my heart, I'd deal with it. I just need to know. "But...if I hadn't, would you still like me?"

"No." My eyes squeeze shut in agony. "When I say you forced your way in, I mean I needed you to. And you did. I'm grateful for it. I wouldn't have given you any chance if you came up to me and asked me out on a date"

My expression loosen immediately, my heart refilling with emotion. I scooch myself into position to hold her tight, burying my nose in the top of her hair.

It isn't long before her breathing became deep and even. I keep her wrapped up, watching her sleep. The apartment is completely silent.

That is, until something begin clanking around in the hallway.

At first, I ignore it, assuming a neighbor is making too much noise as they turn in for the night. But it continue, and it starts to sound a lot more like someone is fumbling with my door. Rage begins to rumble in my chest. Can't a guy watch his girlfriend sleep in peace?

I slide out of bed slowly, ensuring I don't wake Gisele, and creep to the door. Before I can even reach it, it creaks open, and a man I've never seen in my life walks in. Followed by four other men. The lights of the city lit the living room enough for me to see the barrel of one of his guard's handgun pointed at my head.

Well, shit.

His sharp eyebrows angle down. He hasn't even bothered to cover his face. I hold my hands out to the sides and begin to speak quietly. Quietly enough that I wouldn't wake her, but not so quiet that he'd suspect there is someone over there sleeping.

If he found her and hurt her, I would absolutely lose it.

"Who are you?" I ask. There is no way Dylan actually sent someone, and I made nice with all my collectors. I sifted through my mental files, filtering through the never-ending images of Gisele accumulated over the past week, and found nothing of this man.

They might be here because of-

"You're son of Luca?"

My father. I assumed right. These two were the only possibilities. Although, it isn't happening for the first time.

"Who even is that?" I ask.

"Luca Steinfeld."

"I don't know that man. Now leave my house"

"Don't act smart. I saw the nameplate on door"

"You fucking stupid or what? Can't two people have same last name?"

"No matter how hard you and your father try, you can't hide your identity"

"Why don't you directly go to him and ask who his son is?" I say, only mildly sarcastically. They know they would pee their pants if they do that. That's why they're here, for an easy way to connect with him and take revenge of something he did 20 years ago.

That's the biggest pain in the ass in this industry, some random son or grandson of a gangster would come to you after decades, with guns, and take revenge. You can't ever be clean for so long even after you leave this cult, sooner or later you will have to kill to live.

Instead of a response, he cocks his gun.Fine. So my charm isn't going to work this time.

I shift my hand to my back to reach for gun but then realise I kept it in the locker. Shit.

I won't be able to handle them if they're loaded with guns and I'm not.

Suddenly, a smirk falls on my lips looking at the door behind them, "Dad!"

They turn around and I launch onto two of them and disarm them easily, the guns get tossed on the couch. They both fall down on the floor.

Before other two could load their guns, I jump onto them too. Obviously, they charge me, and I send them stumbling back with a kick. I end up in hand-to-hand combat with two of them, as I've intended, punching and whirling around the apartment, kicking other two men when they try getting up. We knock over photos and smash into windows.

As we twist and turn in our tussle, I catch sight of the bedroom. The sheets are moving. My gift is waking up. I beg the heavens she'd keep her fucking head down.

# 20

## Chapter 20

G ISELE

A noise jerks me awake. It takes a minute for me to come to. My head throbs from the sudden jolt, and my eyes only see blurs. It isn't until I realize the spot on the bed next to me is empty that I really perk up.

Where is Heath?

The raucous in the living room area quickly catches my attention, and I watch two men ram Heath right into the tall windows in the dim city light. I gasp, slapping a hand over my mouth.

Heath seems to be winning, so I stay low, creeping off the bed and padding over to the walk-in closet. I place myself inside, able to peek into the living room area from my position.

Grunts and groans fill the apartment when, suddenly, I hear a gunshot.

My heart lurches, my body going numb. I just got Heath back, and I find myself begging the universe not to take him from me so soon.

I can't see where the shot lands, but both Heath and the man pause their tussle, looking toward the front door of the apartment, which is outside my line of vision. There's two more men. Four in total.

Heath slowly untangles from the man and puts his hands up in surrender. He glances at me for only a second. That glance breaks my heart. There's nothing I can do to help.

"You're coming with us," says the new intruder.

I watch wide-eyed as the first man grabs Heath by the T-shirt and shoves him toward the door. As they near the exit, I creep further out to catch glimpses.

Heath trips and falls into the kitchen counter before dragging himself up and following the two men out. The door slams, and I'm alone.

Seriously? What is this, a fucking movie? I finally find a guy who's committed to me and fucks me right, and he gets fucking kidnapped?

My heart bottoms out. What the fuck am I supposed to do? I consider calling the cops but quickly remember Heath is a fucking criminal.

My hands grow sweaty, my chest heaving. I blow air out of my lungs in tight whooshes as I walk out to the living room and ensure the door is shut and locked. It's my fault. If I didn't make him put the gun inside the locker, he would have handled them. I put his life at risk by taking away his security from him.

Phone. Where's his phone? Maybe I can call his friends who work with him. Fran and Noel.

I flick a couple lights on and look around for a full minute, desperately digging in the couch cracks. Nothing. I run back to the room, tossing pillows aside. Fuck, fuck, fuck. Where the fuck is it? I can't find my phone either.

Then I remember. I saw it on the kitchen counter. I look on the bar, next to the stove, behind every appliance. I got it, he placed next to the sink after getting water post-sexcapade.

I stare at his phone for a few long seconds, the puzzle pieces coming together. Oh my god, that sly fucker. I grab the device and click it awake. His screensaver is a picture he stole from my Instagram.

"Fucking weirdo," I mumble, tapping on the glass and preparing to guess the passcode.

But there isn't one. The phone simply opens up to an array of apps. I click through each, unsure of what I'm looking for until I find the one I need.

I launch it and turn up the volume, then I'm listening in on my own phone. The asshole tripped into the counter on purpose and stole my cell. What a smart fucking man.

I'm straining to make out any sounds that might hint at where they're headed when I realize this app can probably track as well. I click around more and open a screen that looks like a map, my phone a little red dot moving along it. I practically jump for joy.

I open his contacts list. And tap of Favorites to see if he has any contacts in that category. Surprisingly, he has.

Asswhole, Dad, Fran, Giada, Mom, My Sweet Gift.

Whoa. Who do I call?

I call Fran but his number is unreachable. And who the fuck is this Asswhole? Should I call his Dad... No. I'll pee in pants by the way Heath described him.I have to make my decision quickly.

I call his mom and she picks up after a couple of rings. "Hello? Is this Mrs. Steinfeld speaking?"

"Who is this?" she asks. Her voice very confident and tone straight to the point.

In the next minute, I find myself running to my suitcase, I rip it open, pulling on black jeans, combat boots, and a tighter sweatshirt that doesn't flail around me. I hurry to the kitchen and grab two of Heath's kitchen knives—the smallest ones in the stand. They look good, probably expensive, but hell, I need something.

"Thanks, Heath," I whisper, stuffing the makeshift weapons into my boots. Before leaving the house and doing what his Mom told me to to, I take out his gun from the locker and keep it with me. Surprisingly, his locker wasn't locked either. Is this guy okay?

My eye catch a handful of bullets inside it too, which I snatch and pound into my back pocket.

I share mine and Heath's location to his Mom quickly as I run down the hallway.By the time I get into a taxi, the red dot on Heath's phone has stopped moving. I spit out the general direction to the driver, begging him to step on it, and flick back to my Google search.

I swipe through loads of articles and forums about helpful gun safety, reading through them quickly, and come to the crushing realization that, without a model, it's impossible to give proper instructions on how to use it.

Fuck.I navigate back to the search bar: Kinds of guns.Scroll ing through pictures, I find one that kind of looks like the one I have tucked into my waistband. Deciding it's something like a Glock 26, I type in my original question again, desperately trying to figure out how to load the fucking thing.

There are fucking YouTube videos on it. Seriously? I laugh a bit, thinking back to Heath telling me he learned how to tap phones on YouTube. I thought he was joking, but now, I'm not so sure. I visualize the process enough times with the video on silent and decide I'll wait until I'm out of the taxi to load the weapon. This taxi driver certainly doesn't need to be involved in whatever the fuck I'm about to walk into.

I type in a new search: How to throw knives.I figure it could be useful. I find another YouTube video. Naturally. I watch the technique of the man in the video, taking obvious note of the fact that I have kitchen knives, not throwing knives, and the mechanics are probably totally different.

But, hey, something is better than nothing. I observe the position of the man's wrist, the way he tosses the knife with enough force but not too much, and how he aims. "Easy enough," I murmur to myself, though it's a fucking lie. I have most certainly gone around the fucking bend. I can't even believe what I'm on my way to do. All I know is that I need Heath back. He's mine, and they took him from me. We finally arrive at a freaky brick building, and the taxi driver asks me twice if I'm sure this is the spot before finally accepting payment and leaving me alone. The streets are eerily empty, the moonlight bouncing off the slick pavement.

Okay, Gisele, you just have to trust your instincts will kick in or something and you will finish them all. I look back, I should wait for his Mom. But if it's too late by the time they reach here? She told me she is not too close to us, but she will try reaching as soon as possible. Also told me not to put myself in danger.

But what if they're about to kill him?!

I should try to keep those men with him busy until help reaches us. Like they do in movies, chatting about random stuff to keep the villain occupied. I stalk around the side of the building, trying to pretend I'm in an action movie to take the edge off, doing everything I can to forget the fact that I'm holding a gun and that, pretty soon, some guys will likely be holding guns at me. Milky windows dot the sides of the building; some are partially shattered, others only cracked.

I keep walking until I find one that's broken enough to work with. Picking off the giant shards, I break the glass as quietly as I can, carving a hole big enough to hoist myself through. With much difficulty, I swing a leg through the opening and burrow my way into the building, pieces of window scraping through my jeans as I go.

The abandoned halls inside the building are vaguely lit by the streetlamps outside. I pull out Heath's phone, attempting to will my shaky hands to still, and turn on the flashlight, keeping it faced down to the ground.After walking about five minutes, I see a faint stream of light entering the hallway, and I know I must've found them. I shove Heath's phone into my pocket and hold the gun up the same way I've seen cops do it in TV shows: arms bent up, gun by the side of my head.

I have no fucking idea why I'm meant to hold it that way, but it seems like a decent attack position.Creeping around the corner, I let only my eyes peek into the lit room. And there he is. Under a lanky lamp in the middle of a wide-open room, Heath sits tied to a chair by his wrists and his feet, and there's rubble tossed around him.

Well, there's rubble everywhere. The place is a shithole and completely deserted.

Two other men are in the room with Heath. I hope they're the only two on the job and that a third won't come jumping out from behind me.

I desperately hope someone is on their way to help. I'm not that good at chatting, keeping a criminal occupied in my talk.

The taller of the two men paces in front of Heath, twisting a knife in his hand."We are trying to contact your father. If he doesn't come, he can say goodbye to his son" he says, inspecting the tip of his weapon as he walks."You still haven't told me who you're with," Heath answers, his head hanging tiredly to one side, blood trickling from his brow underneath his bent glasses. "And to be honest, this trick has been played by many before.

Many times. And all of them had their balls chopped off by my father, and hands cut off by my mother. She keeps it easy."He is trying to scare them Maybe it is working."Look, I'm gonna make this simple..." The man approaches Heath and dips the tip of his knife into his thigh. Heath groans, but his smile grows wide, his eyes taking that crazed look they often do. He almost looks like he likes it. I smile to myself. Sick fucker.

"First, I'm going to kill you. If that doesn't light a fire under your father's ass, I will kill his wife. And his daughter. And his sister. I have gotten a huge amount in exchange of making a deal with him in exchange of you, and that I can't miss."Heath laughs, which makes me grin even wider. "If you want the job done faster, you should kill off the weakest link. Not the strongest and most handsome one."

The man pushes the blade deeper into Heath's leg, and Heath grits his teeth, yelling in his throat. The man's face a look of disgust, "What kind of man are you? Throwing such shitty jokes about your family's death?"Heath gives him a sweet look, "That's because I know my father will lit you on fire alive even before you lay a finger on my family"

Mmm. Is that so.

In a perfect world, where there's no guilt, no consequences, and I have excellent aim and precision, I would simply send a bullet to the taller one's head and another to his accomplice's directly after.But, alas, I'm not even sure the gun will fucking shoot correctly. For all I know, I've shoved the bullets into the wrong compartment, and it's about to combust in my face. Fuck, I wish Heath were untied. Then he could help me.

I watch the blood from his thigh drip beneath the hem of his gray sweatpants. He's still in his pajamas, shoeless, and probably freezing. The floor beneath him is quickly turning red, and I know I have to do something. Fast.I decide on maiming instead of killing, maybe shooting a calf or an arm. I figure that'll be easier on my conscience. Besides, I can just pretend it's Dylan.

I wait until the taller man has paced far enough away from Heath that I won't accidentally kill my little damsel in distress should my shot go awry, prepare as I've seen done in the YouTube video, and take a shot.

My shoulders jerk back far more than I expect them to, and my ears fucking scream. But, by some small miracle, I've managed to shoot the guy. Where? I'm not entirely sure, but one of his legs collapses, his own gun sputtering across the floor from beneath his clothes as he falls.

Heath's eyes snap to me as the smaller man jumps into action, grabbing the gun off the floor and running toward me, firing shots in my direction. Fuck, fuck, fuck! I hide behind the wall, too terrified of the barrage of lead to step back out and take another shot. Instead, I reach down to my boot quickly and pull out one of Heath's kitchen knives.

I remain crouched, hoping the guy might come around the corner looking for me and that I'll win a split second before he looks down and finds me. He does, and I do.

His body turns in search of me, and before he can figure out where I've gone, I jam the knife into the side of his thigh, practically gagging at the feel of it slicing in. He punches my face and fall back. I guess he hit my nose hard. It's bleeding."You motherfucker!" Heath hisses.Suddenly, the man is holding a gun on my head.

There's nothing I can do now. I look at Heath helpless, raising my arms and surrender in fear."Leave her!" Heath shouts but then suddenly smirks, "Because they're here"

Just then, a shot fires behind me, and a bullet sinks into the man's head. I scream at the sight of him going down.

"She's fine, fuckface!" I whip my head around to find two men approaching along with a woman in black outfit and a gun. Along with her, there's one in a plain, black ski mask and another in one with a different variation of a skull from Heath's. They're Fran and Noel. Thank God.

They're still hiding their identity. But the woman isn't hiding anything. She... she looks like Heath. She's his Mom. She looks so fit, confident and aged finely. I don't know how to put it into words, but... she just looks so ready to break bones right at this second. Heath told me she is a martial arts expert, maybe that's why.

It adapted into her look.Noel runs past me to the room where Heath sits while Fran helps me up. "Are you okay?" Heath's mother asks me."I- I'm fine but..." I look back Heath and run to him."Baby," Heath breathes, eyes wide and smile gleaming. "There were only two of them? Go check around here, and shove these men into the car. We need answers" his Mom commands as more men run inside, with damn big guns in their hands as if they're starting a war. At least we don't need to worry even if there's more men ready to fight us.

"Who the fuck are you?!" Fran and Noel try getting answers from the men on floor."Don't chop off anything yet, my girl isn't fond of butchering" Heath tells him. And he is serious. For a second, I believe everything he said all this time was true.

"Thanks for helping my son" his mom comes, looking directly at me while I'm just sitting against Heath and clutching his leg. She smiles at me, "But who are you?"

"Your daughter in law, Ma" Heath says quickly. I look at him, at his large blue eyes, at his boyish grin. I let out a shy laugh.S uddenly, his mom's phone rings and she picks up, "Everything is fine. You don't need to come, babe." she looks at me and smiles sweetly, as if she already likes me, "And there's a good news, I'll tell you about it when I get home."

When things settle a little, I tie his wound with a cloth to stop it from bleeding. He caresses my hand and pecks my lips. I missed him so much. "You got me so worried." "I'm sorry, baby" he pecks my lips again.Noel comes to check on us. "Who are you?" he asks me."My fucking girlfriend" He grins. Once again."I'm his fucking girlfriend" I repeat after him and his grin gets even wider.

**21**

## CHAPTER 21

H EATH

Oh, fucking fuck, I was gonna come in my pants right fucking there. Iwanted to hear her say it again and in that exact fucking tone. I wanted to watch her go feral to protect me just as I would her. She held a gun in each hand like they were pieces of too-hot toast.

Like she wanted to touch them as little as possible, dangling them between two fingers.

It was hands down the cutest fucking thing I've ever seen in my life.

And totally not the proper way to handle a firearm. She was going to shoot someone by accident if she kept it up.

"Ask her who she is," I urge, piled into the back of our windowless van with Neil and Gisele, Fran at the wheel. Mom left with guards from right there as she had some important work.

Neil groans. "I've already asked her like four fucking times, dude."

"Who are you, Gisele?" Fran calls happily from the front.

"I'm his fucking girlfriend!" she says with a giggle, crashing her cheek to my bare shoulder. I grin wide as the horizon and drag her from her seat and onto my lap.

Suddenly, a sharp pain shoots through my entire body as her ass hits my thigh, and I remember. That fucking asshole stabbed me. It'll probably be a couple weeks before I can even fuck my girl properly.

"Oh, babe, be careful," she says, plucking herself off of me and avoiding my thigh.

My anger melts instantly. I'd take a hundred more stab wounds if it means Gisele will keep accepting me this way.

I peek forward at the windshield to find that the sun is just starting to rise, the spots of sky between the skyscrapers turning a deep purple-pink.

We're headed in the direction of my organization, but, truthfully, I just want to sit in the shower while Gisele and I wash each other and then curl into bed together.

She's only been moved in for like nine fucking hours, and already two people are dead, more are going to die, I've been stabbed, and she's somehow learned how to use a gun.

We've hardly even gotten to just snuggle up.

"That doesn't happen all the time, does it?" she asks quietly, peering up at me with her chin on my shoulder bone. "The abduction and the killing?"

I don't want to lie to her.

"No, my sweet gift." I smile and kiss her on the nose. "It won't happen again. I will break their bones if anyone tries touching you. My mom also said she will send us few guards, if you're so concerned. But, please let me keep gun in case-"

"I'm sorry, I shouldn't have made you put the gun away..."

Oh no. She shouldn't be sorry at all. Her comfort matter the most. "Your presence scared me. I got scared if they catch you, they will hurt you. And I lost it. I will do better. I promise." I tell.

I hold out my little finger, and she hooks hers in mine. She seems satisfied with that and returns to leaning on my shoulder.

When we arrive at the organization, I sling my arm around her as we hop out of the back of the van. She props me up to walk inside, and I guide her to my office, where she helps me sit in the chair behind my desk.

Fran spins off to grab some simple supplies and returns to dress my wound properly and wipe the blood off my face.

It's hardly 7:00 a.m. When my leg is finally patched and everyone is done fawning over me, I stand with my girlfriend. There's someone very important she has to meet.

Max lays in the corner of his private playroom, chin over his paws as we enter. His fluffy head perks up at our arrival, and it makes my heart melt. My little guy—well, big guy—is so strong and so brave.

Gisele slaps her hands to her mouth and squeals, jumping up and down in place. "He's so cute," she whispers.

I quirk an eyebrow. I've never seen her so jumpy and giddy before. Why doesn't she get that way when she sees me? I humph and pull her tighter to my side.

"Just remember he's sick and tired. He's been going through treatment, so he's a little grumpy lately." She wraps her arms around my waist as we walk towards my dog slowly. "Why isn't he home?"

"He's been staying here the last few weeks," I say, gesturing around the room we've prepared for him with a bed, blankets, and toys. "It's more comfortable. Fran and Neil stay here, taking care of him. I've just been so busy, and he likes it here."

"That's so sweet."

Stepping just in front of Max's paws, I crouch down and give him a pat on his black-and-white back. "Hey, boss."

He releases a worried little grunt but hardly looks at me. His eyes are fixated on Gisele.

My smart, composed girl, whose walls stand so high, gets down on her knees, then lays on the floor on her stomach, and puts her nose in front of Max's. Max makes another little sound and boops his nose to Gisele's. My heart combusts at the sight.

She nuzzles her face into his fur and plops her head down on the floor by his foot. He rests his chin across the side of her head, and I immediately reach into my pocket for my phone. I find Gisele's instead and make a mental note that we should swap back eventually.

"New lock screen," I say, snapping a picture.

Gisele giggles. "Better than stealing my photos from the internet."

I thump my ass down on the cold floor and snuggle in with her as best I can. Max moves his head around to try and rest it between us.

"You were amazing tonight, baby," I say, staring sideways into Gisele's beautiful gray eyes. "I could hardly believe it was you when you took that first shot."

She smirks. "You underestimate me."

"Gisele..." I place a hand on her freckled cheek. "I worship you."

Gisele touches her fingers to my jaw and leans into me for a slow kiss. For a few moments, we are simply wrapped in bliss, our lips sliding together as we lie tangled on the floor.

A wet nose on my cheek interrupts us, and Max refuses to let us continue, sticking his snout between our faces and demanding our attention.

Gisele leans up and kisses him on the cheek, and he makes a happy little noise.

"In a couple hours, our staff will get in," I say, smiling as I watch her and Max play together. "We can take everyone out from their cages and bring them to the playroom if you'd like. We can nap in my office until then."

She gets confused and looks around. "What do you mean staff? Cages? Where are we?"

I smile, she still doesn't know many of the things going on.

"This is a small veterinary clinic. One of the things I run around this city with Fran, he is a veterinarian. Gyms and bars were boring ideas of my father, so I invested in this. I don't get much profit from it but I don't need it either. I should declare it a free service already."

# 22

## EPILOGUE

H EATH

6 Months Later.

I am sitting on the couch of our apartment, sprawled with my legs wide and feet planted on the floor. Butt ass naked. A movie dances on the TV screen, snacks piled high on the white table, and the walls around me are nothing but windows to the dark city. This is the only fucking place I ever want to be. My heaven.

Gisele is in the kitchen refilling the dog bowls. We brought a little Italian greyhound puppy home that Max used to keep an eye on at the organization. Gisele calls her Noodles. And Max has been in a significantly better mood since his another surgery. I think it has relieved a lot of his pain.

After finishing with the bowls, my naked, little Gisele stalks back over to the living room area, and my head falls to the side so I can catch every inch of her from every angle.

She stands there, mindlessly bunching her hair in her hand, watching the TV screen for a few moments. My tongue drags across my bottom lip as my eyes eat up that ass, the curve of her lower back, the way her hips sway naturally every time she moves.

My dick begins to harden, standing up on its own, my arms thrown over the back of the couch. My gaze trails up to my girl.

"Gisele," I sing, "please come sit on my cock, baby. I'm begging you."

She rips her attention away from the TV screen and glances over her shoulder at me, her teeth peeking through those full lips.

"I don't know," she says, sauntering toward me slowly. "Are you sure you deserve it?"

She places a hand on each of my knees and presses her weight into her palms, kneeling in front of me.

"Yes," I whimper. "Please, my sweet gift. I'll do anything."

"Anything?"

"Anything."

She smiles and leans in, placing her pink tongue at the head of my cock. She wraps that wet, little thing around my skin, and my head falls back into the cushion behind me. It's delicious, but it's not enough. I desperately need more.

She pulls her tongue in and trails her lips down to the base of my cock, her hot breath hitting my skin the whole way down. A long lick up the underside of my dick has my hips grinding.

"Don't move," she scolds.

"Aaah," I groan, my cheeks stretching back into a grin and a little chuckle escaping my throat. Oh, how I love my wicked girl.

She tortures me with soft, barely-there touches that have me coming undone. I am completely helpless to her. Finally, her hot, wet lips take me fully, sliding down my shaft over and over again.

Fuck, my life is perfect. This is everything I've been waiting for. She is everything I've been waiting for. My friends adore her, and so does Fran's wife. I've never seen Gisele with a friend before, but in the last few months, she has grown quite close to his wife, and I am overjoyed to see it.

My family also loved her. Yes, she met each one of them. And the first thing she said in my ear was -- "Your Dad isn't that scary."

I laughed it off. Oh baby, you haven't seen.

I'm happy she loved each one of us. Especially considering she'll be joining the family soon.

When I am mewling with pleasure, begging my girl for more, she finally pops her mouth off with a slurp and lifts herself over me, sinking that sweet pussy down on my dick. I moan and move my hands from their perch on the couch to receive her, holding her beautiful body between my palms as she gets comfortable.

Digging my thumbs into her stomach, I run my hands roughly over her skin. It's vital that I feel every single atom that constitutes her physical form.

My eyes trail lazily from her belly button up to the space between her tits, which bounce just as she does. I devour the sight of her collarbone and her neck, finally landing on my favorite fucking thing: that beautiful face.

I practically come when her eyes lock on mine.

"I love you, Gisele." I've told her quite a few times already, though she hasn't said it back yet.

Each time, she just rolls her eyes and tells me she'll let me know when she believes it. I have a feeling she's starting to come around, and I wait desperately for the words to fall from her lips so I can finally fucking propose to her.

"Heath," she whines, sitting down hard on my cock, letting it hit her deeply. "Heath." I listen to her moans as she bounces on me faster. "I love you, Heath."

My eyeballs practically fall out of my head. My heart is a supernova.

I grab her quickly and circle my fingers around her clit, forcing her to come hard as quickly as possible. Not that I don't want her to take her time and enjoy it, but I can't hold myself together after hearing her say that. I blow in an instant as she grips me tight, sucking me into her.

I let us both sit there, breathing heavily for a few seconds, before launching off the couch and picking her up with me. She hangs on me like a monkey, my cock still inside her and my cum starting to drip down our skin as I run to the bedroom.

"Heath!" she squeals. "What are you doing?"

It is finally time. It is finally fucking time. We are comfortable and in love.

I fumble around in my nightstand drawer in a rush, holding her with one arm, until I find the little black box. Turning myself to sit down on the edge of the bed, I leave her straddling me and open it in front of her.

"You're my greatest gift, baby. Please marry me. I'm begging you to marry me."

She tilts her head back and laughs, and I fall even more in love.

"It took me this long to tell you I love you, and the second I do, you move right along to marriage?"

"Yes," I blurt before the final syllable can leave her mouth.

"Don't you think it's too soon?"

I cock my head. "You mean like when it was too soon to move in together?"

"Kind of like that," she says with a smile before grabbing my hair in her hands and crashing her lips to mine. She pulls away for only a moment to say, "Yes."

"Yes?" I breathe, my chest glowing and warm.

"Yes."

I push the ring onto her finger, joy flooding my senses as I continue to bite at her delicious lips. Standing and flipping her around, I lay her out on the bed, my cock growing inside of her again already.

www.ingramcontent.com/pod-product-compliance
Lightning Source LLC
Chambersburg PA
CBHW071013180726
48291CB00004B/1438